NICKELODEON

SpongeBob™ SquarePants

Survival Guide

BY David Lewman

D1115805

POCKET BOOKS

New York   London   Toronto   Sydney   Singapore   Bikini Bottom

An *Original* Publication of POCKET BOOKS

 POCKET BOOKS, a division of Simon & Schuster, Inc.
1230 Avenue of the Americas, New York, NY 10020

ISBN: 0-7434-6987-9

First Pocket Books trade paperback printing November 2002

10 9 8 7 6 5 4 3 2 1

For information regarding special discounts for bulk purchases, please contact Simon & Schuster Special Sales at 1-800-456-6798 or business@simonandschuster.com

Book concept by Tricia Boczkowski
Shark photo by Carl Roessler/Getty Images
Design by Red Herring Design/NYC

Printed in the U.S.A.

CONTENTS

INTRODUCTION...7

Chapter One: SPONGY SURVIVAL..........................9

How to Tell If You're Ready.....................................**11**
How to Spot a Fake Sponge....................................**12**
How to Tell If You've Absorbed Too Much Liquid...............**14**
How to Hide in a Grocery Store.................................**15**
How to Treat a Plugged Hole....................................**16**
How to Survive Drying Out......................................**19**

Chapter Two: BRINY SURVIVAL..........................21

How to Open a Giant Clam.....................................**22**
How to Tell a Joke to a Shark...................................**24**
How to Tame a Wild Jellyfish....................................**26**
How to Deflate a Puffer Fish....................................**29**
How to Control a Runaway Seahorse..........................**30**
How to Chase Down a Runaway Snail..........................**33**

Chapter Three: KRUSTY SURVIVAL.....................35

How to Make a Krabby Patty...................................**36**
How to Handle a Rush at the Krusty Krab.....................**37**
How to Rescue a Fallen Krabby Patty..........................**40**
What to Do If You Lose Your Spatula...........................**42**
How to Avoid Doing Work..**44**

Chapter Four: NEIGHBORLY SURVIVAL.....................47

How to Be an Excellent Neighbor...**48**
How to Create Privacy...**50**
How to Karate-chop a Squirrel..**52**
What to Do If Your Bubble Helmet Runs out of Water................**54**
How to Survive a Whirlpool...**56**
How to Survive a Secret Crush..**58**
How to Win a Snowball Fight...**59**
How to Survive a Skiing Trip..**61**
How to Tell When You've Blown Too Many Bubbles...................**62**
How to Motivate a Starfish..**63**

Chapter Five: NAUTICAL SURVIVAL...........................65

How to Escape from a Floating Boat..**67**
How to Swab a Deck...**68**
How to Drop on the Deck and Flop Like a Fish.........................**70**
How to Avoid Being Struck by Falling Anchors.........................**71**
How to Fix a Broken Bike Paddle...**72**
How to Deal with Being Covered in Algae................................**74**
How to Survive a Pirate Attack..**76**
How to Remove Barnacles (from Yourself)...............................**77**

Chapter Six: SCHOOL SURVIVAL.................................79

How to Survive a Pop Quiz......................................81
How to Survive Art Class..82
How to Survive Gym Class.......................................84
How to Survive Being on a School Team.................86
How to Win a Race...87
How to Tell If a Bubble Likes You............................88
How to Survive a School Dance................................90
How to Deal with a Bully...92

Chapter Seven: HOUSE SURVIVAL..............................93

How to Tell If Your House Is Rotting.........................94
How to Treat a Severed Limb....................................95
How to Get out of Bed...96
How to Deal with Sleep Deprivation..........................98
How to Tell When It's Time for a New Shell...............101
How to Survive a Haunting.......................................102

Chapter Eight: FINANCIAL SURVIVAL......................103

How to Protect Your Money......................................104
What to Do with a Treasure Chest............................107
How to Foil a Fast-change Scam Artist.......................109
How to Ask Your Boss for a Raise..............................111
How to Put Your Archrivals out of Business (Unsuccessfully).....113

Chapter Nine: WILDERNESS SURVIVAL..............115

How to Find Your Way to the Krusty Krab
without a Compass...116
How to Find Your Way out of an Undersea Cave.....................118
How to Survive Being Lost in a Kelp Forest............................121
How to Find Water in the Ocean...122
How to Survive Being Lost in Your House.............................123

Chapter Ten: DANGEROUS SURVIVAL..............125

How to Escape from a Pool of Tartar Sauce............................126
How to Survive Being Hooked..128
How to Survive an Underwater Volcano Eruption...................129
How to Escape from a Bubble..131
How to Survive Tripping...133
How to Survive Ripping Your Pants..134
How to Survive Being Bare..135
How to Survive Waiting in Line at the Movies........................136
How to Survive Needing to Go to the Bathroom....................138

HOW TO END A BOOK..............139

ABOUT THE SPECIALISTS..............140

iNTRODUCTiON

B Y SpongeBob SquarePants

Wow! Survival is great! I love survival! Gonna survive! Gonna survive! Gonna keeeeeeeeeeeeeeeep on survivin'!

But it's not easy. Life at the bottom of the sea is tough. It's dangerous. It's wet. Does that frighten me? No way! Because I know how to survive!

And you can, too! At home. In school. At work. Even in the clutches of Man Ray and the Dirty Bubble! You can do it! I know you can! When you know how, surviving is as easy as flipping a Krabby Patty. It's downright simple!

Everywhere I look, I see survivors. Patrick, Squidward, Sandy, Gary, Mr. Krabs—they're all surviving! Of course, they know a thing or two about survival. That's why some of these survival secrets are by them. Secret secrets—the secret kind that are so secret I secretly can't tell you how secret they are, secretly.

Follow these step-by-step instructions, and you'll be like me—porous, yellow, and totally unsinkable! Well…unsinkable, anyway. And you'll survive! Oh, yeah, you are gonna survive like crazy! Ready? I am! I'M READY! I'M READY! I'M READY! I'M READY!

—SpongeBob SquarePants

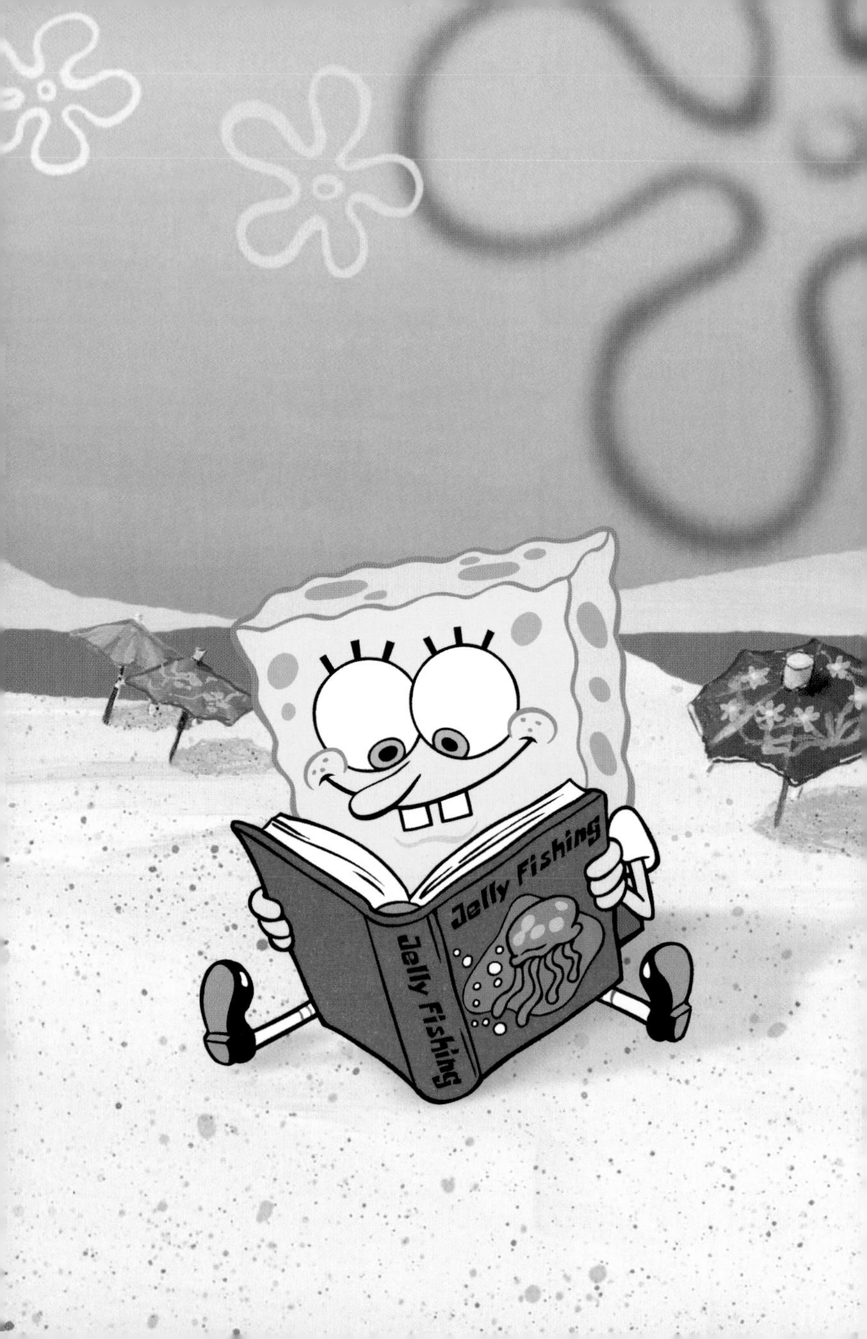
Jelly Fishing
Jelly Fishing

CHAPTER I:
SPONGY SURVIVAL

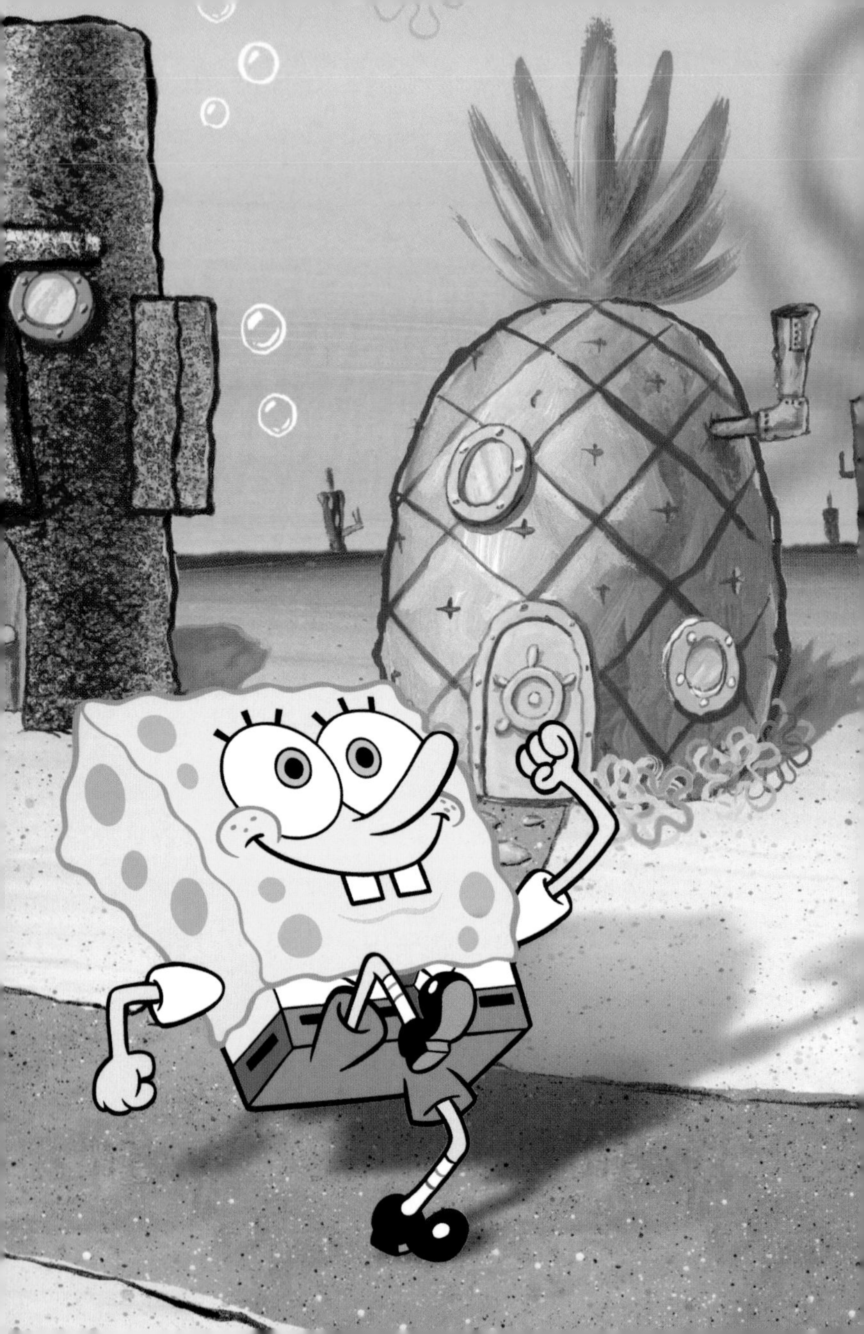

HOW TO TELL
iF YOU'RE READY

BY SPECIALIST SpongeBob SquarePants

1 Do you feel ready? Concentrate on your stomach and try to get a reading on your gut feeling. If you don't feel ready, right in the middle of your body, you may not be ready. Or you may have made the mistake of eating at the Chum Bucket.

2 Check for signs of unreadiness. Are you in some way unprepared? Unqualified? Unwilling? If you see even the slightest hint that you are not ready, you may not be ready.

3 Ask a friend. Go to your best friend in the whole world, wake him up, and say, "Patrick, do I look ready to you?"

4 Try saying it. Whisper, just once, the words, "I'm ready." How did that feel? Good? Accurate?

5 Say it louder. "I'm ready!"

6 Repeat it over and over as you march out of your house. "I'M READY! I'M READY! I'M READY!"

7 You, my friend, are READY! Unless you've forgotten something.

HOW TO SPOT
A FAKE SPONGE

Be Aware

Sponges are about the most popular creatures in the sea, so naturally lots of people try to pass themselves off as sponges. But if you pay attention, you can always tell a phony sponge from the real deal.

NOTE: *Not all sponges are yellow* (just the best-looking ones). Therefore, just because a sponge isn't yellow doesn't mean it isn't real.

1 Spill your drink. Then say, "Oh, gee, do you think you could soak that up for me?" A bona fide absorbent sponge will have no problem passing this little test.

2 Ask to see his membership card from the International Association of Sponges.
If he shows it to you, he's a phony. There *is no* International Association of Sponges.

3 Spill an even bigger drink.
He may have had a towel hidden in his pocket the first time.

4 **Say, "You know what's fun? Ripping yourself into tiny pieces and then putting yourself back together."**
If you're a sponge, do it first, to show how fun it is. Once you've put yourself back together, you'll probably find that the fake sponge has taken off for parts unknown. If you're *not* a sponge, bet him a Krabby Patty he can't do it. A real sponge will tear himself apart in a second for a delicious Krabby Patty.

HOW TO TELL IF YOU'VE ABSORBED TOO MUCH LIQUID

1 You can water the plants in your yard just by walking over them.

2 Instead of shaking your hand, people wring you out.

3 You could really go for some dry crackers, popcorn, and salt packets.

4 After your friends hug you, they immediately have to put their clothes in the dryer.

5 Nobody can tell when you're crying.

6 The fire department runs hoses out of your head.

7 When you try to step inside your house, your foot fills the living room.

HOW TO HIDE IN A GROCERY STORE

BY SPECIALIST SpongeBob SquarePants

1 Head for the cereal aisle. One of the best places to hide is behind cereal boxes. Especially yellow ones. (If you're yellow!)

2 Or the aisle with the soap. Mix in with the boxes of laundry detergent.

3 Or the cheese section. A great place to hide! But a little chilly.

4 Do not hide in a freezer case. Your chattering teeth will give you away.

5 Or with the cleaning supplies. You may accidentally get bought.

6 Try not to giggle. People know that cereal boxes and blocks of cheese don't giggle, so they'll get suspicious.

7 Keep in constant communication with your best friend Patrick via walkie-talkie. Unless he's the one who's looking for you.

Be Aware
While shopping for groceries, you may realize you're being followed. Or you may see a bully. Or you may get the urge to play hide and seek. You need to HIDE!

HOW TO TREAT A PLUGGED HOLE

1 **Determine what is plugging the hole.** A cork? A wad of gum? A Ping-Pong ball?

2 **Do not immediately insert a bicycle pump into an adjacent hole.** Though this seems like the most natural way to fix the problem, it's not the first method you should try.

3 **Apply pressure to the area around the plugged hole.** With your hands. Do *not* use pliers. Or a vise. Or one of those big wooden nutcrackers that looks like a crazy soldier with giant teeth. Why do you even own one of those creepy things?

4 **Elevate the plugged area.** If possible, stand on your roof.

5 **Apply butter to a stack of pancakes.** The butter can be melting while you're working on unplugging the hole. When you're done, you can have a delicious breakfast!

6 **Put on your reef blower.**

7 **Set your reef blower on "reverse."**

8 **Turn on your reef blower and stick the end in the plugged hole.** Whatever's plugging the hole should come right out!

9 **But if it doesn't, keep vacuuming while you use a bicycle pump on an adjacent sponge hole.**

10 **Enjoy your pancakes!**

How to Avoid Plugged Sponge Holes

★ Never take a tour of a cork factory.

★ Never swim in tar.

★ Be careful when playing with marbles.

★ Before you play in a box, dump out *all* the packing peanuts.

★ Never challenge Patrick to a game of tiddly winks.

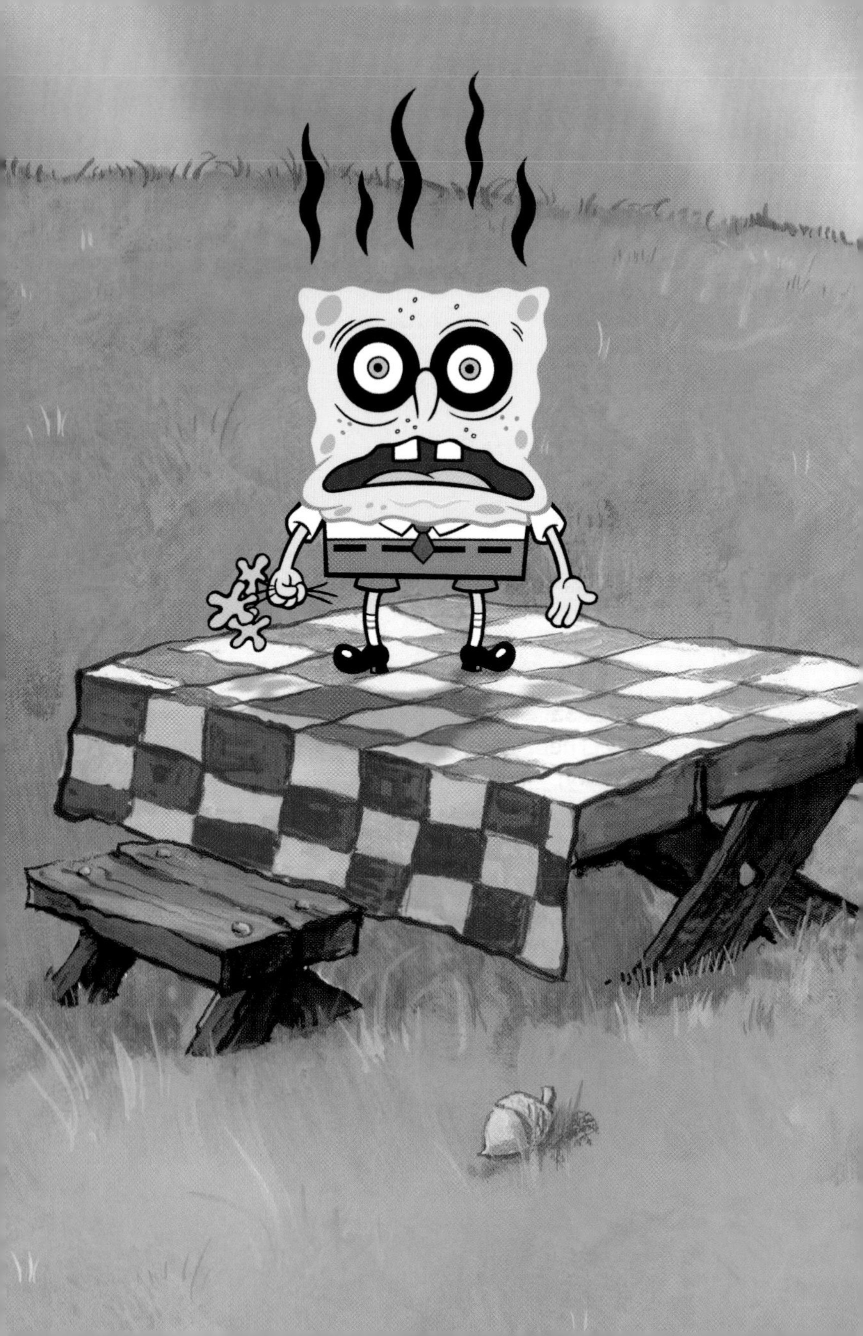

HOW TO SURVIVE DRYING OUT

1 Check for water under your tongue. This is one of the last places to dry out. Stick your finger under your tongue, and then try to spread the moisture over your body.

2 Don't cry. No matter how upset you are about drying out, you don't want to lose water in the form of tears. If you do cry, try to cry into a cup. Then hold the cup upside-down over your head.

3 Look around to see where you are. If you're drying out, chances are you're in one of two places: out of the ocean or in Sandy's treedome.

4 If you're out of the ocean, get back in the ocean. Remember: the ocean is the blue stuff with waves on top.

5 If you're in Sandy's treedome, get out of there immediately. There'll be plenty of time to thank Sandy for a fun visit later on. Right now, you're seconds away from turning into a piece of toast—with no jelly.

6 Once you're back in the water, take your clothes off. You want to expose every porous inch of you to liquids. But first, make sure no one can see you. When you're all shriveled up and desiccated, you don't really look your best.

7 Blink. If you hear that nice wet *bloink bloink* sound, you're okay.

8 For the next couple of days, don't wring yourself out.

Signs You're Drying Out

★ When you try to talk, dust comes out of your mouth.

★ All of a sudden, your clothes are way too big.

★ You smile and your mouth falls off.

★ Your new nickname is "Sahara."

★ Sandpaper feels slimy to you.

★ You're so thirsty, you'd actually drink vegetable juice.

How to Avoid Drying Out

★ When the ocean starts getting really shallow, turn around and go back to the deep end.

★ Always carry a spare swimming pool.

★ Never take your bubble helmet off in Sandy's treedome, even if your nose itches.

★ Drink plenty of fluids, except for vegetable juice. It's wet, but it tastes horrible.

★ Stay home on sunny days.

CHAPTER TWO:
BRINY SURVIVAL

HOW TO OPEN
A GiANT CLAM

From the Outside

1 Knock on the shell. This will get the clam's attention.

2 If you have a giant clam opener, use it.

3 If you don't have a giant clam opener, go to a store and buy one. Then use it.

4 If all the stores are closed or out of giant clam openers, look for an "Open" button on the clam's shell. If you find the button, push it. The clam should pop open.

5 If you don't have a giant clam opener and you can't find an "Open" button on the giant clam, look around for something to pry the giant clam open with. Possible things to use: a crowbar, a stop sign, a diving board, a samurai sword, the world's largest popsicle stick.

6 Stick the prying thing in between the top shell and the bottom shell. Push it in as far as you can.

7 Jump up and down on the prying thing.
If it's a diving board, this will be fun. If it's a samurai sword, it won't be. Eventually, the giant clam should open. Or the prying thing will break.

From the inside

1 Don't knock on the inside of the shell to get the clam's attention. You're trying to sneak out. You want the clam to be thinking about something else besides you.

2 If you have a flashlight in your pocket, take it out and turn it on. Don't light a match. This will only annoy the giant clam.

3 Find the clam's "tickle spot." It's not labeled. It's just the part of the clam that looks the most ticklish.

4 Tickle the clam's tickle spot.
Using your fingers, make a light, rapid tickling motion.

5 When the clam opens its mouth to laugh, jump out.

Be Aware
None of this
will work
on a giant
oyster.

HOW TO TELL A JOKE TO A SHARK

1 **Make sure it's not a shark joke.** They don't like those.

2 **Make sure it's not a lawyer joke.** For some reason, they don't like those, either.

3 **Don't be distracted by the shark's teeth.** Remember, you're trying to make the shark laugh— you *want* to see his teeth. Though you don't, of course, want to feel them.

4 **Find out if the shark really wants to hear a joke.** Start off with a simple, "Hey, wanna hear a joke?" You don't want to try to tell a joke to a shark who's not in the mood to hear one.

5 **Speak clearly, and don't go too fast.** You don't want the shark to miss part of the joke and start thinking about something else, like a feeding frenzy.

6 **Stay calm.** Sharks can sense nervousness from up to four miles away. Of course, if you're telling the shark a joke you should probably be a little closer to it than that.

7 **Do funny character voices.** Sharks love that.

8 **Don't insist on telling the joke from inside a shark-proof cage.** This tends to insult the shark.

9 **Before you start, be sure you remember the punch line.** Actually, this is a good idea no matter who's hearing the joke.

Three Kinds of Jokes Sharks Like

SEAL JOKES are sure-fire winners with sharks. They never seem to get tired of laughing at seals. Or eating them.

LIGHT BULB JOKES are very popular with sharks for some reason. If you can come up with a joke about Steven Spielberg screwing in a light bulb, you've got it made, shark-wise.

"A FISH SWIMS INTO A CAVE..." jokes rarely fail with sharks. If you're telling the joke to a Great White, make it a big fish.

Be Aware

Almost any large shark, roughly six feet or longer, is a potential non-laugher. As the old saying goes, "the bigger the shark, the smaller the laugh." Three species in particular are known to be laugh-killers: the white shark *(Carcharodon makemelaughas),* the tiger shark *(Galeocerdo Ibetuthinkurfunnius),* and the bull shark *(Carcharhinus idongetit).* When telling jokes, avoid them at all costs.

HOW TO TAME A WILD JELLYFISH

Be Aware

A wild jellyfish is wild—that's why it's called a wild jellyfish. You don't want to just toss a leash on one and bring it into your home. (You'll end up with jelly *every-where.*) If you really want to tame a wild jellyfish, you have to be willing to put in some time.

The First Year

1 Visit the jellyfish in its native habitat every day. But don't look directly at it. In fact, for the first eight months, you should always turn your back toward the jellyfish. For the first three months, you shouldn't even be there.

2 In your twelfth month of visiting, start to leave tiny plates of food for the jellyfish. But don't watch it eat.

Years Two Through Five

1 Continue to bring small amounts of food to the jellyfish every day.

2 Gradually start to watch the jellyfish eat.

3 In the fifth year, from a distance of at least half a mile, try waving at the jellyfish.

Years Six Through Fifteen

1 **Every day, move the plate of food one inch closer to your house.**

2 **In years ten through fifteen, start to call the jellyfish by name.** Start with just the first letter of the name, then add another letter every six months or so.

Years Sixteen Through Twenty

1 **To make sure everything's okay, move the plate of food one inch *away* from your house every day.**

Years Twenty-one Through Twenty-five

1 **Move the food very gradually back toward your house.**

2 **In years twenty-four and twenty-five, make a soft, pure-silk leash one strand at a time.** Let the leash lie on the ground within sight of the jellyfish's plate of food.

Years Twenty-six Through Thirty

1 **Continue to greet the jellyfish by name.**

2 **If it wants to, let the jellyfish sting you repeatedly.**

3 **Every day, move the plate of food a fraction of an inch toward the leash.**

Year Thirty-One

1 **Slip the leash around the jellyfish.** For the last year or two, the jellyfish has been eating from a plate inside the leash. It should now be a fairly simple matter to gently lift the leash up around the jellyfish.

2 **Slowly lead the jellyfish into your house.**

Years Thirty-Two Through Fifty

1 **Train your jellyfish to be housebroken.**

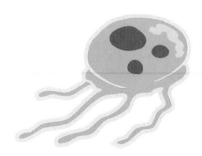

HOW TO DEFLATE A PUFFER FISH

BY SPECIALIST Mrs. Puff

1 First, try to make the puffed fish comfortable. If SpongeBob is present, remove him immediately. Then give the puffed fish a pillow and a blanket. Some chocolate would be nice, too.

2 Delicately make sure you're not just dealing with a fish who's fat. Do NOT say, "Now, you're not just *fat*, are you?" Try something like, "My, what made you suddenly puff up?" If the person answers "cake," deflation may not be possible.

3 Tickle the puffed fish's feet. This will begin the deflation process.

4 While the P.F. is giggling, gently open the valve at the back of his or her neck.

5 Don't open the valve too fast. You don't want the puffed fish to fly around the room.

6 Don't leave the valve open too long. The puffed fish's clothes will give you a good indication of how big the fish is supposed to be when deflated.

7 Do NOT stick the puffed fish with a pin! That's just cruel. And besides, the bang will be deafening.

8 While the deflated puffer is recovering, do not let SpongeBob anywhere near a boat.

HOW TO CONTROL A RUNAWAY SEAHORSE

if You're Riding the Seahorse

1 Say to the seahorse, "Hey! What's your hurry? Where are we going?" If you're lucky, the seahorse will realize it has nowhere to go, and will slow down.

2 If the seahorse still doesn't stop, try to steer it toward a stop sign. Seahorses are generally reluctant to break the law.

3 If the seahorse blasts through the stop sign, take a Krabby Patty out of your pocket. You should always carry a Krabby Patty when you go seahorsebackriding. That way, if the seahorse gets out of control, you can hold the Krabby Patty behind you, waving its delicious smell toward the seahorse's nostrils. When it smells the Krabby Patty, it'll turn its head around, and try to gallop toward the patty. But since you're on the seahorse's back, it'll end up just running around in a little circle until it stops. Then you can give it the Krabby Patty. Don't eat it yourself. That'll just make the seahorse really mad.

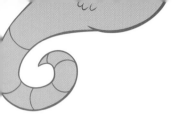

4 **If you don't have a Krabby Patty, grab the seahorse's tail and pull straight up.** If you pull hard enough, the seahorse should be upside-down, and it's very difficult to be a runaway when you're upside-down.

if Someone Else is Riding the Seahorse

1 **Grab the nearest Krabby Patty.**

2 **Jump in front of the seahorse holding the Krabby Patty straight out in front of you.**

3 **When the seahorse stops to eat the Krabby Patty, grab the reins and tell the rider to jump off.**

4 **Remember to let go of the reins before the seahorse finishes the Krabby Patty.**

if Nobody's Riding the Seahorse

1 **Let the seahorse go.** Who wants a seahorse that's going to run wild, anyway?

31

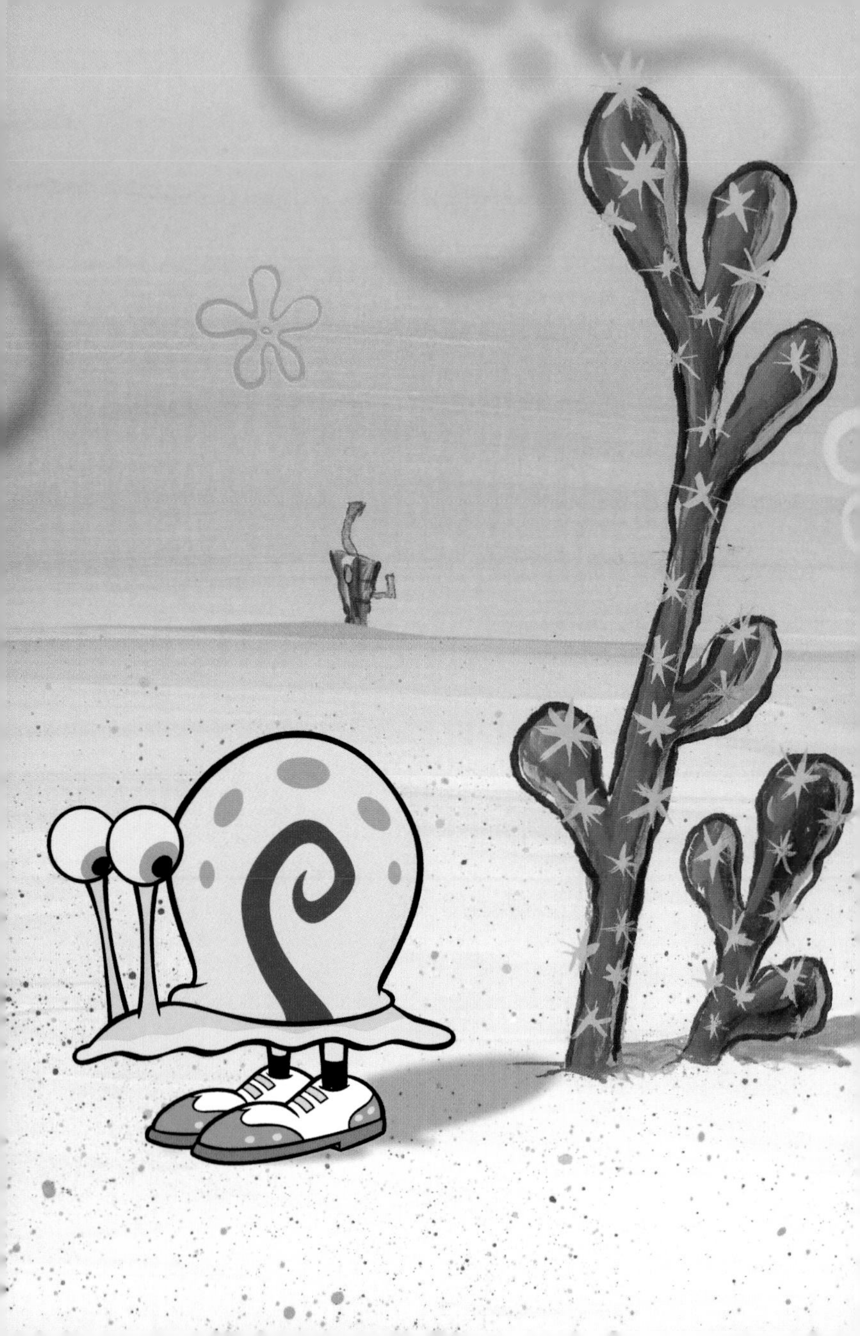

CHAPTER THREE:
KRUSTY SURVIVAL

HOW TO MAKE A KRABBY PATTY

1 Take one patty.

2 Grill it at a hot temperature, for an amount of time.

3 Take one bun.
The buns have two parts, a top and a bottom.

4 Put some... stuff... on the top half of the bun.

5 Using a spatula, slide the cooked patty off the grill and onto the bottom half of the bun.

6 Being careful not to spill any of the... stuff, put the top half of the bun on top of the patty.

7 And there you have it— a delicious Krabby Patty!

8 If you want a Krabby Patty With Cheese, you have to add one more ingredient.
But we can't tell you what it is.

HOW TO HANDLE A RUSH AT THE KRUSTY KRAB

if You're a Customer

1 **No matter how long the line may be, don't go somewhere else.** A Krabby Patty is worth waiting for.

2 **Stay calm.** Eventually, Squidward *will* take your order. Eventually.

3 **Prepare your order ahead of time.** Make your decision quickly (you really can't go wrong), and then repeat it to yourself over and over ("a double Krabby Patty with fries, a double Krabby Patty with fries, a double Krabby Patty with fries..."). After a while, it will start to sound like nonsense to you, but keep repeating it.

4 **Put Squidward in a good mood.** When he's trying to deal with a rush, it can't hurt to say things like, "Boy, I sure do love modern interpretive dance" or "To my way of thinking, the clarinet is the king of instruments." You might even get extra ketchup.

5 **While you're waiting for your food, pick out a table to eat at.** During a rush, all the tables will be taken, but watch for these signs that people are about to leave:

★ Crying—people get very sad when they realize they've finished their Krabby Patties.

★ Sighing while saying sentences like "Gee, I really want to eat more Krabby Patties, but if I do my body will explode."

★ Kissing—of the table, not each other, while saying, "Good-bye, table, I'm really going to miss you."

6 The second you get your food, sprint to the table you've picked out. But DON'T DROP YOUR FOOD! That would be a tragedy almost as horrible as the daily special at the Chum Bucket.

if You're an Employee

BY SPECIALIST SpongeBob SquarePants

1 A really big rush at the Krusty Krab is the ABSOLUTE GREATEST!

2 You get to do your job, only you get to do it even more! And faster!

3 So the real danger is in getting too excited. You have to stay calm and focused.

4 But that's pretty much impossible, because the more customers, the more Krabby Patties, which is VERY EXCITING!

5 YAY!!!!!!!!!!!!!!!!!!!!!!!

6 OH, BOY—LOTS AND LOTS OF CUSTOMERS!

7 WHICH MEANS LOTS AND LOTS OF KRABBY PATTIES!

8 THIS IS THE EMPLOYEE'S TIME TO REALLY *SHINE!*

9 Unless you're Squidward. Then you complain a lot.

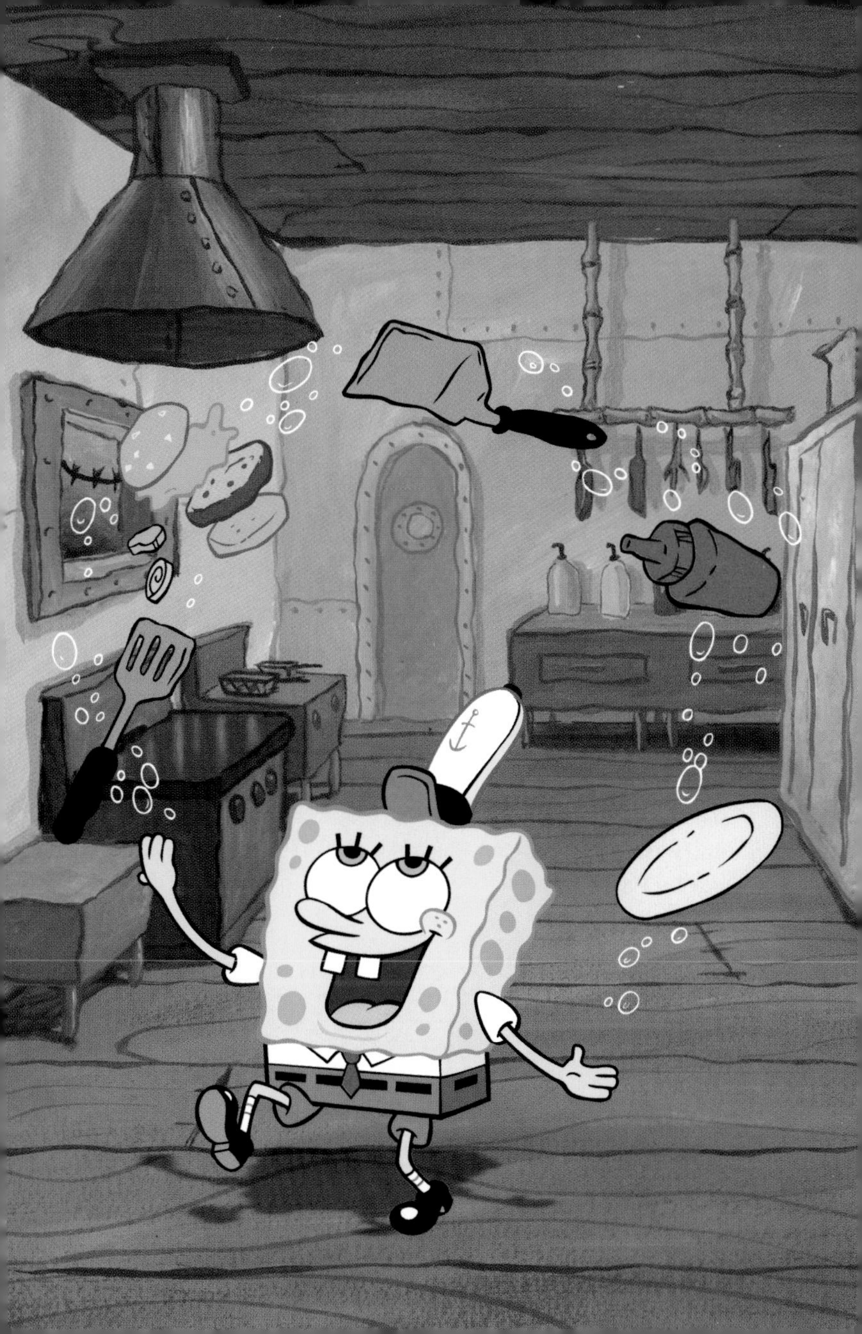

HOW TO RESCUE A FALLEN KRABBY PATTY

1 **The second you see the Krabby Patty start to fall, dive to catch it.** You can eat off the floors at the Krusty Krab, but you don't want the Krabby Patty to be bruised.

2 **If you're too late, and the Krabby Patty's already on the floor, use both hands to gently pick it up.**

3 **Slowly turn the Krabby Patty in your hands, all the way around, checking for injuries—a torn bun, a slipped patty, a fractured pickle.**

4 **Don't let the Krabby Patty see how upset you are.** It'll only worry the Krabby Patty. Flash your biggest smile and say, "Don't worry, little patty. You're going to be all right!"

5 If the bun's damaged in any way, replace it with a fresh bun.

6 If there's anything wrong with the patty, replace that, too.

7 While you're at it, you might as well replace all the other ingredients.

8 And there you have it—a rescued Krabby Patty, good as new!

How to Avoid Dropping a Krabby Patty in the First Place

1 **Go into the Krusty Krab kitchen.** Go on in—they've got nothing to hide! (Except the money, which Mr. Krabs hides in the safe. And his desk. And his pockets. And under his tongue.)

2 **Stand by the fry cook waiting for your Krabby Patty to finish cooking.**

3 **As soon as the cook has assembled the Krabby Patty, ask him to please slide the Krabby Patty right into your mouth.**

4 **He'll be happy to do it!**

5 **Remember, chew before you swallow.** Unless you're Patrick. Then it doesn't seem to be necessary.

WHAT TO DO iF YOU LOSE YOUR SPATULA

BY SPECIALIST SpongeBob SquarePants

1 Don't flip out! That's a little fry cook humor. But seriously, it seriously is a serious situation when you lose your spatula, so you seriously want to stay cool, calm, and seriously collected. Try to get a handle on the problem. (HA HA HA HA HA! That's a little more fry cook humor.)

2 Try to remember where you last had your spatula. In the kitchen? In the shower? At the beach? I never travel without mine, so it could be almost anywhere.

3 Check the ground for spatula tracks. If the ground around you looks as though it's been patted down and then flipped, a spatula's been there.

4 Ask your friends. You should probably just keep repeating, "Has anyone seen my spatula? Has anyone seen my spatula? Has anyone seen my spatula?" until it shows up.

5 Check that junky drawer in your kitchen full of weird utensils.

6 Put up a poster. The poster should say "Has anyone seen this spatula?" under a picture of your spatula. Make sure it's a recent photo.

7 Offer a reward. No amount is too high to get back your spatula. Well, except maybe more than the price of a new spatula.

8 Look for clues. See anything that's been turned over? Squished? Chopped up? That just might be the work of a stolen spatula.

9 **Set a trap.** Put a patty on a grill. Now hide. Leave the patty cooking on *one side only*. No matter how done it gets on that side, *do not* turn it over. This will be hard to watch. Eventually, whoever took your spatula will run in, crying, and flip the patty over with the missing spatula. At least, that's what I'd do.

Substitute Spatulas You Can Use Temporarily Until Your Real One Turns Up

★ A flyswatter

★ A Ping-Pong paddle

★ A gardening trowel

★ A paintbrush

★ An oar

But a better option is simply to lift the stove and flip your patties that way. Remember: it's all in the wrist. And the back.

HOW TO AVOID DOING WORK

BY SPECIALIST Squidward Tentacles

How to Hide From the Boss

1 Learn what sounds your boss makes when he's moving around. Maybe yours whistles. Or hums. Or talks to himself. Mine talks to his money.

2 Listen carefully for the sound of your approaching boss.

3 As your boss approaches, get out of sight. Climb under your desk. Crawl under a rock. Squeeze into the cash register. Just find a place where you can't be seen.

4 Wait for your boss to go away. Even if one of your four legs starts to cramp, don't move.

5 When you hear your boss going back into his office, stay put. It might be a trick.

6 When you're absolutely sure he's gone, emerge from hiding. And be ready to duck right back into your hiding place on a moment's notice.

How to Get Your Coworker to Do the Work For You

1 If your boss gives you an assignment, call your coworker over. Whether it's taking out the garbage or mopping the floor, you shouldn't have to be the one to do it.

2 Pretend you don't know how to do the chore.
Act as though you really *wished* you knew how to do it,
but you just don't.

**3 Ask your coworker if he or she knows how to do the
chore.** If your coworker is SpongeBob, you probably won't even
have to ask.

**4 After the coworker explains how to do the task,
pretend you still don't get it.**
What you need from your
coworker is a *demonstration.*

**5 Once your coworker has
done the work for you,
pretend you *still* don't get
how to do it.** That way, you can
ask him or her to show you how
again the next time.

Be Aware
Don't worry about having
your coworkers think
you're stupid. It's better
to be thought of as an
idiot than to get garbage
on your hands.

How to Leave Work Early

**1 Bet your coworker that he or she can't do his job
and your job.**

**2 Tell your boss that because of a special union rule,
if you stay any longer he'll have to pay you quadruple
overtime.**

**3 If your boss still says you can't leave, set the clocks
forward while he's not looking.** You'd be surprised how
often this works.

4 If the clock trick doesn't work, just sneak out.
Your boss might yell at you the next day, but what else is he going to do? Fire you? No one else wants your lousy job.

How to Quit Forever

1 Think of a much better way to make money, like joining a symphony orchestra as the star clarinetist.

2 Stride purposefully into your boss's office and say, "I QUIT FOREVER!"

3 Don't leave immediately—you want to remember the look on his face.

4 Dance your way out of there, singing and laughing as you toss your ridiculous uniform in the trash.

5 Never, ever go back. Unless the orchestra thing doesn't work out.

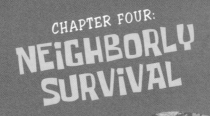

CHAPTER FOUR:

NEiGHBORLY SURViVAL

HOW TO BE AN EXCELLENT NEIGHBOR

BY SPECIALIST SpongeBob SquarePants

Be Aware

It's not easy being an excellent neighbor, but
I feel very confident that I have mastered the fine
art of neighborliness (just ask Squidward).
By following these few simple steps, you can, too!

1 Get to know your neighbor. Before you can be an
excellent neighbor, you have to know just who it is you're
living next to. Introduce yourself.
Talk to your neighbors
every single day!
If they won't come
to the door, just
keep calling until
they do!

**2 Include your
neighbor in your
activities.** If you're playing
a game in your yard—
from "Toss the Paint Can"
to "Foghorn Freeze Tag"—
invite your neighbor to join
the fun!

3 Participate in your neighbor's activities. If your neighbor's doing something, you should do it, too! For example, when your neighbor starts playing his clarinet, grab a handy instrument, like a washboard or a gong, and play along. Follow his lead—if he starts playing louder, you should play louder, too!

4 Tear down fences. Let your neighbor know he's free to come and go in your yard whenever he wants. You can set a good example by playing in his yard whenever you feel like it. He'll get the idea before you know it!

5 Don't be too formal. With a neighbor, you can be casual. If you want to tell your neighbor something, you don't have to call him on the phone or ring his doorbell, you can yell through his window. Yelling though someone's window gives him a warm, neighborly feeling.

6 Share your food. If you fix way too much food, and you just can't eat it all, and it's starting to go bad, don't throw it out—give it to your neighbor!

7 Share your pet. Let your pet wander into your neighbor's yard whenever it wants to. That way, your neighbor will know that *"mi pet es su pet."*

8 Connect your houses. For true neighborliness, dig a tunnel connecting your basements, or build a breezeway between the upper stories. For some reason, Squidward hasn't agreed to this one yet. He's probably just worried about invading my privacy. But he shouldn't be. I don't believe in privacy. That's what makes me such an *excellent* neighbor!

HOW TO CREATE PRIVACY

BY GUEST EXPERT Squidward Tentacles

1 Put more locks on your doors. You really can't have too many. I like to say that good locks are the *key* to privacy. Get it? Key? Heh heh. I'm hilarious.

2 Soundproof your house. Attach corkboard, Styrofoam, mattresses, and pillows to the walls of your house with marshmallow paste. Of course, that still leaves the windows. I'm thinking of having mine removed.

3 Consider blocking up your chimney. Sure, fireplaces are nice, but at what cost? You can always get an electric one.

Be Aware

Some people just don't get it. You want to be left alone, to enjoy your solitude, to relax in your house with a good book and a cup of tea. But they *refuse* to leave you alone. They're *constantly* bugging you. That's when you have to take things into your own hands. You have to create your own private privacy.

4 Build tiny secret rooms.
With a few false walls and
panels, you can add secret
rooms to closets, kitchen cabinets,
and toilet tanks. Of course, I'm not
going to tell you where *mine* are.
Let's just say there are over forty of
them, and so far SpongeBob's
only found thirty-nine.

**5 Get an unlisted phone
number.** Better yet, get an
unexistent phone number.
Who needs phone calls?

6 Build giant fences around your house.

7 Have your mail delivered to a post office box.
It's well worth having to go to the post office to pick it up.

8 When you go to the post office, wear a disguise.

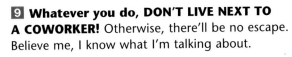

**9 Whatever you do, DON'T LIVE NEXT TO
A COWORKER!** Otherwise, there'll be no escape.
Believe me, I know what I'm talking about.

HOW TO KARATE-CHOP A SQUIRREL

What You'll Need

★ Protective headgear

★ Protective handgear

★ A squirrel

1 Put on your protective gear. Karate is a recreational sport, so you don't want to unleash the lethal weapons that are your bare hands. Plus, without gloves you'll get a big owie.

2 Sneak up on the squirrel. Squirrels are excellent at defending themselves, so the element of surprise is crucial. Gather all the squirrel's friends in one room, turn out the lights, and wait for her to walk in so you can all jump up and yell, "Surprise!" Wait—that's for a birthday cake, not a karate chop. Anyway, um…sneak up on her.

3 Leap through the air. As you leap, let out a big karate yell. It'll ruin the element of surprise, but it helps focus your karate energy. Plus, it's fun.

4 Aim for a soft spot. Of course, since squirrels are covered in fur, they're pretty much just one big soft spot. So basically just avoid the teeth.

5 Chop with your strongest hand in a swift chopping motion, thumb-side-up. If you try to chop thumb-side-down, you're liable to dislocate your elbow. And hurt your thumb.

6 Prepare to be blocked. Remember how in Step Two above we didn't really tell you how to sneak up on the squirrel? And how in Step Three we said to yell? She knows you're coming.

7 Fly through the air in the opposite direction. Because you've just been counter-chopped by a squirrel.

WHAT TO DO IF YOUR BUBBLE HELMET RUNS OUT OF WATER

1 **Do not panic.** Well, you can panic a little if you want to. The panic might even get you to solve your problem faster. So, on second thought, go ahead—panic!

2 **Signal that you need more water by flailing your arms wildly.** Whoever's in charge of providing water (probably Sandy) will pour new water in your helmet, and you'll be fine.

if Sandy Doesn't Notice Your Signal

3 **Flail your arms *and* your legs.**

4 **If necessary, throw something at her.** When she turns to look, flail like crazy.

if Sandy's Hibernating or You're All by Yourself

5 **Rub your face around the inside of the helmet to soak up every last drop of water.**

6 **Look for a source of water.** Sources of water include: hoses, buckets, bottles, glasses, pitchers, vases, gutters, troughs, ponds, rivers, springs, watermelons, leaky basements, and the ocean.

7 **Crawl to the source of water.** You want to conserve your energy. Also, if anyone happens to see you, it looks a lot more dramatic.

8 Yank off your bubble helmet. Be careful not to drop it. If it smashes into a million pieces, it'll be really hard to refill it with water.

9 Pour the water in your helmet. Don't waste time looking for ice cubes.

10 Plunge your head into the water-filled helmet.

11 Stand up with your helmet back on. Soak it in for a minute or two, then quickly make your way home. Once you're there, you can sit around drinking plenty of liquids. And you won't need a helmet.

Be Aware

If Sandy's hibernating, DO NOT wake her up and ask for help. Hibernating squirrels are far more dangerous than leaky bubble helmets.

HOW TO SURVIVE A WHIRLPOOL

BY SPECIALIST Sandy Cheeks

1 **The first thing to do when you realize you're in a whirlpool is to yell, "YEEEEHAAAAAW!"**

2 **Next, y'all want to jump up onto your board of choice: boogie, surf, snow, or even ironing.**

3 **Try to stay at the top of the whirlpool as long as you possibly can.** One good way to do this is to surf up *out* of the whirlpool—and then immediately dive back in!

4 **Once you've swirled around in the direction of the whirlpool a couple of hundred times, flip around and try going *against the direction of the whirlpool*.** Opposite whirlpooling ROCKS!

5 **Stick your hand into the cone of water and see how high you can send it fountaining *above* the whirlpool.** Again, you might want to say, "YEEEEHAAAAAW!"

6 **Invite all your friends to join you.** The only thing better than whirlpooling is whirlpooling with friends!

7 **Eventually, slide down to the bottom of the cone of water.** Jam your board in the bottom of the cone and spin like a top. Talk about speed!

8 **To be fair, some people think whirlpools are dangerous.** Those people are NO FUN!

if the Whirlpool isn't Going Fast Enough

1 **Position yourself right at the top of the whirlpool.**

2 **Lie down on your board.**

3 **Kick and paddle as fast as you can, staying in the circle of the whirlpool.**

4 **This should speed the whirlpool up.** YEEEEHAAAAAW!

5 **'Course, the whirlpools are much bigger and faster in Texas.**

HOW TO SURVIVE A SECRET CRUSH

BY SPECIALIST SpongeBob SquarePants

1 The most important thing about a secret crush is that it stay secret. Super secret! Super DOUBLE secret! Super TRIPLE secret!

2 You can't tell anyone! Not even your best friend!

3 And especially not the person you have the secret crush on.

4 You have to act natural around your crushee. Don't giggle. Don't go weak in the knees. Don't blush. And don't fog up your bubble helmet. (Wait a minute—forget I said that last part.)

5 Take me, for example. I act perfectly natural when I go over to the treedome and…

6 I'VE SAID TOO MUCH!

HOW TO WIN A SNOWBALL FIGHT

BY SPECIALIST **Patrick Star**

1 **Get SpongeBob to make you a snowball.**
A big one.

2 **Throw it in his face.**

3 **HA HA! I WIN! I WIN!**

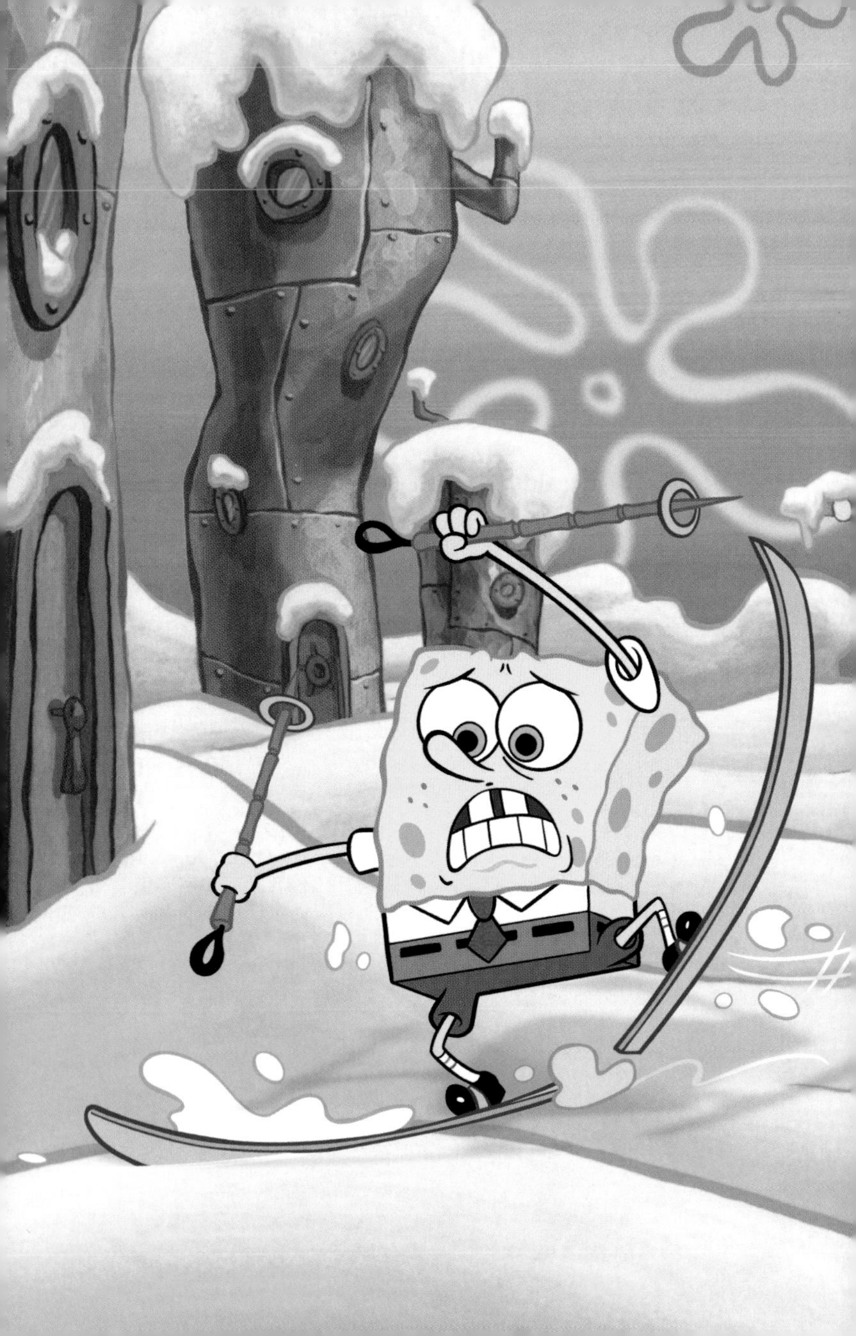

HOW TO SURVIVE A SKIING TRIP

1 If your neighbors invite you along on a skiing trip, say "Sure! I'd love to go!"

2 On the way to the slopes, tell everyone what a great skier you are.

3 Once you get there, rent the fanciest equipment you can find. Tell everyone you need this stuff for speed.

4 Let everyone hear you ask where the most dangerous trail is. Find the "double-death black skull" run.

5 Go up to the top of the killer run.

6 Take off all your equipment and carefully crawl down the back way.

7 Hang out in the lodge saying how exciting it was.

Be Aware
If Sandy comes along on the skiing trip, this won't work. She'll insist on skiing the killer slope with you.

HOW TO TELL WHEN YOU'VE BLOWN TOO MANY BUBBLES

1 Neighbors ask if they can wash their dishes in your mouth.

2 The only words you can say all end in "ooooo."

3 You've got a bad case of "wand hand."

4 You don't even bother to sit up anymore, so they just float down and pop on your face.

5 People are starting to call you "the guy who spends every waking moment blowing bubbles."

6 You've sold everything you own to buy more bubble solution.

HOW TO MOTIVATE A STARFISH

1 Be really clear about what you want the starfish to do. If you're at all vague about what you want, the starfish will use that as a reason to do nothing.

2 Put it in writing.
Starfish are excellent readers (they love to spend all day lying around with a book—usually on it), so if you *write down* what you want them to do, they can't pretend you never told them.

3 Hand the instructions to the starfish *directly*. Otherwise, they'll say they never got them. In fact, they still might.

4 Be very clear about deadlines. If you're not specific about when you want the job done, the starfish will put it off until tomorrow. And when we say tomorrow, we mean sixteen years from tomorrow.

5 Don't threaten the starfish with punishment. Starfish don't respond well to threats. Threats make them sleepy. So does punishment. So does breathing.

6 **Do offer an incentive.** Yes, starfishes can be bribed. They all have their price. It's just a matter of finding out what they want, and offering it to them.

7 **Be positive.** Jump up and down and cheer something like, "RAH RAH RAR! GO, MISTER STAR! RAH RAH REE! THE BEST IN THE SEA!"

8 **Praise the starfish each step of the way.** Don't be afraid to say things like, "Way to go! You opened your eyes!" and "All right! You're moving!"

CHAPTER FIVE:
NAUTICAL SURVIVAL

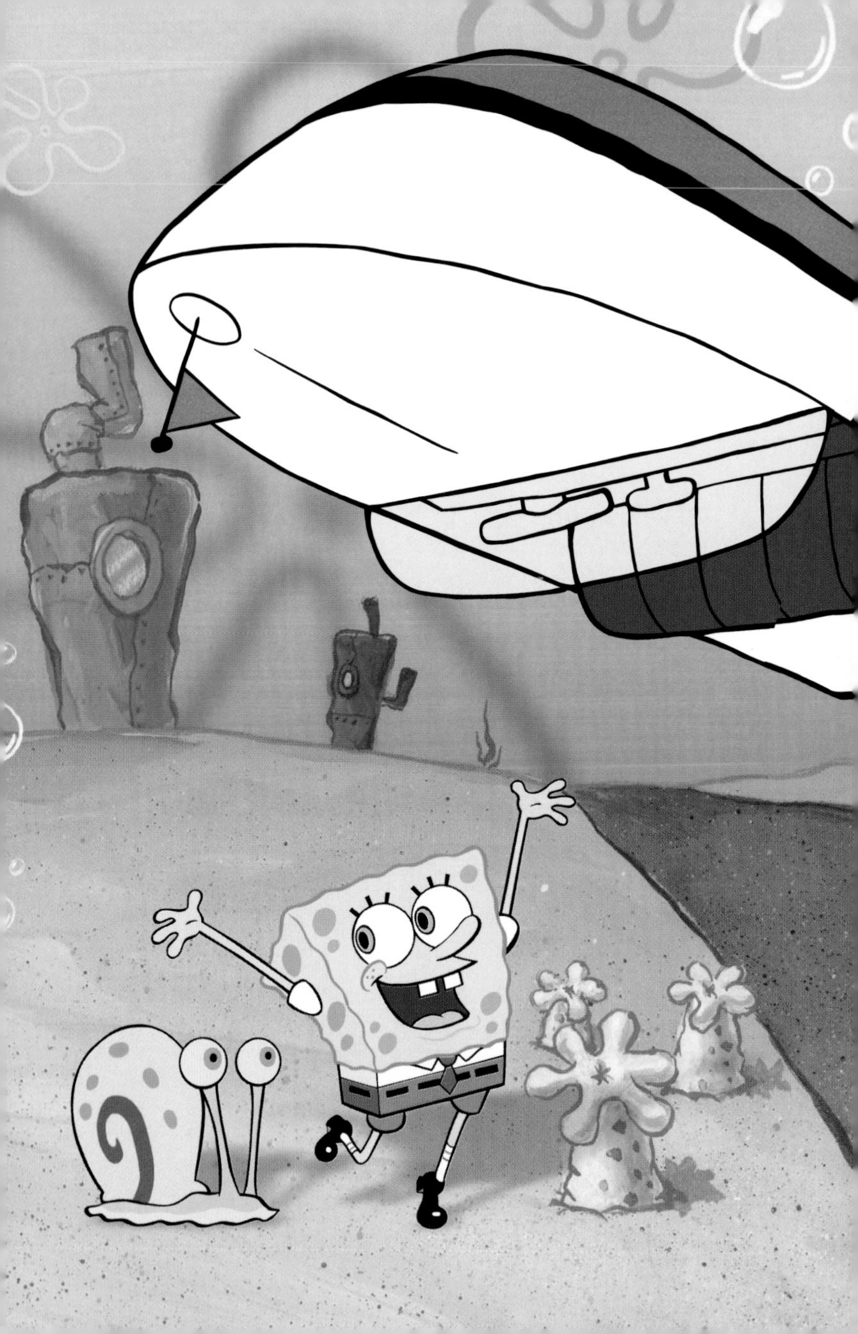

HOW TO ESCAPE FROM A FLOATING BOAT

1 If your boat suddenly starts to float up toward the surface, do not panic.

2 Take your hands off the steering wheel. It's impossible to jump out of a boat while you're holding onto the wheel. Unless you have extremely long arms.

3 Unfasten your seatbelt. You should always wear a seatbelt. Unless you're trying to jump out of your boat.

4 Grab your removable seat cushion. In most boats, your seat cushion can be used as a nonflotation device.

5 Climb up onto the side of the boat. Do not waste time opening the door. Or getting your sunglasses out of the glove compartment.

6 Leap out of the boat! Hug the seat cushion to your chest, and you should sink safely down to the bottom of the ocean.

Be Aware
If your boat is floating upside-down, you can skip steps five and six.

HOW TO SWAB A DECK

BY SPECIALIST SpongeBob SquarePants

Be Aware

What some people call "mopping the floor," Mr. Krabs always calls "swabbing the deck." I don't know why. I think he used to play a lot of cards. At first he taught me how to swab the deck, but eventually I developed my own special method!

1 Don't use those cotton swabs made for cleaning your ears. They do a pretty good job, but they take forever.

2 Prepare yourself. Run around the deck yelling, "Gonna swab! Gonna swab! Gonna swab! Gonna swab that deck!" for an hour or two.

3 Prepare the deck. Run around the deck yelling, "Gonna swab you! Gonna swab you! I'm gonna swab you, deck!"

4 Fill the buckets. That's right, buck*ets,* not bucket. For real swabbing, you need one bucket of water for every four square inches of deck. Once you've begun swabbing, you won't have time to stop and refill a bucket, so you need to fill all the buckets before you start.

5 Add the cleaning solution to the buckets. I like to use a special formula of soap, cleanser, scrubbing agents, glass cleaner, detergent, bleach, floor polish, wax, washing powder, sodium bicarbonate, antidirt flakes, wood solvent, board lotion, nailhead cream, deck purifier, and highgrade, super-grit polishing sand. You should, too.

6 Stir the solution in the buckets. You need to mix the ingredients thoroughly. But not too vigorously, or they'll explode.

7 Pour the entire contents of one bucket onto a four-inch square of deck.

8 Let it soak for eighty-two minutes.

9 Use your body to swab the wet area of the deck. Real swabbing means hurling yourself onto the deck, soaking up as much liquid as you can, spinning like a top, squeezing the excess moisture back into the bucket, slamming yourself back onto the deck, polishing it, and then doing a sort of one-legged backward pirouette across the surface of the deck. Got it?

10 Repeat until you've covered the entire deck. If this takes more than twenty-four hours, you should immediately start swabbing the deck again, since swabbing must be done daily.

11 Enjoy yourself! Swabbing is fun!

HOW TO DROP ON THE DECK AND FLOP LIKE A FISH

Drop on the deck and flop like a fish!

1 **Drop on the deck.** Stand on a deck. Then stop supporting yourself with your legs.

2 **Flop like a fish.** Keeping your arms (or fins) at your side and holding your legs (or tail) together, kick up your feet and raise your head as high as you can. You may also want to open and close your mouth repeatedly.

HOW TO AVOID BEING STRUCK BY FALLING ANCHORS

1 Remember to occasionally glance up.

2 Listen for the sound of rattling chains.

3 If you're directly under a ship, move.

4 If you notice an anchor-shaped shadow quickly growing bigger around your feet, move.

5 If someone yells, "Hey, that anchor's about to drop on you," move.

6 If an anchor-shaped rush of water passes over you, move.

7 Never look up and say, "Nyah, nyah—bet you can't hit me with that anchor."

8 Stop strolling through the Anchor Disposal Dump.

HOW TO FIX A BROKEN BIKE PADDLE

If You've Got a Spare Bike Paddle in Your Pocket

1 Remove the broken bike paddle.

2 Replace it with the spare bike paddle.

If You've Got a Ping-Pong Paddle in Your Pocket

1 Remove the broken bike paddle.

2 Replace it with the Ping-Pong paddle.

If Your Bike Paddle Breaks in a Bicycle Repair Shop

1 Tell the bicycle repairman your paddle is broken.

2 Let him fix it. After all, he's the professional!

iF You've Got Nothing in Your Pocket That Resembles a Bicycle Paddle and You're Nowhere Near a Bicycle Repair Shop

1 **Look around for something stiff that's shaped like a paddle.** A piece of coral, a broken board—even a dried-out seaweed leaf will do.

2 **Pick it up.**

3 **Remove the broken bike paddle.**

4 **Replace it with the paddley thing you've found.**

5 **Ride to the nearest bicycle repair shop.** And prepare to be laughed at for having such a weird paddle.

HOW TO DEAL WiTH BEiNG COVERED iN ALGAE

1 Do not attempt to scrub the algae off.
This will just make the algae mad.

2 Talk to the algae. Pitch your voice high, since this is the tone of voice the algae use to communicate with each other.

3 Find out what they want. Why have the algae attached themselves to you? Shelter? Photosynthesis? Friendship? What's it all about, algae?

4 If it's friendship, consider keeping the algae.
You can *always* use another few thousand friends!
But if you're going to let the algae stay, you should lay down a few rules about how many of them are allowed to live on you and exactly where they're allowed to go. Even friendship has its limits.

5 If the algae are using you for anything besides friendship, persuade them to leave. Point out how much roomier some of your friends are. Say that you don't look good in green, or blue, or red, or whatever color they are. Talk about how much you hate sunshine.

6 If the algae refuse to leave, make a deal.
Convince them to at least arrange themselves to look like a shirt, tie, and shorts.

How to Avoid Getting Covered in Algae

1 Move around. The less rocklike you are, the less likely you are to get covered in algae. Obviously, this is a serious problem for Patrick.

2 Stay in a cold, dark place. Sure, algae can live in Antarctica. And they can live by thermal vents at the bottom of the sea. But they can't live where it's cold *and* dark. Of course, neither can you, for very long, without going bonkers.

3 Make yourself unattractive to algae. Wear mismatched outfits. Don't wash your hair. Don't brush your teeth. Talk too loudly. Monopolize conversations. Talk about yourself constantly. The unfortunate side effect here is that you'll be unattractive to *everyone*.

4 Say insulting things about algae. For example, you might walk into the Krusty Krab and exclaim, "You know, aquatic, eukaryotic, photosynthetic organisms can really be a royal pain in the wazoo!" Of course, this may backfire if the algae decide to teach you how nice they can really be.

5 Dip yourself in a tub of "Algae-B-Gone!" It really works! (Though it smells worse than the grease traps at the Chum Bucket.)

HOW TO SURVIVE A PIRATE ATTACK

1 Pirate attacks can come at any time, so stay sharp.

2 If you notice any of these signs, you may be having an attack of piracy:

★ You have a strong urge to wear an eye patch.

★ You're constantly saying, "aaargh."

★ When you see a parrot, you try to coax it onto your shoulder.

★ You refer to your best friend as "me matey."

★ Instead of carrying your bandana in your pocket, you tie it around your head.

3 **Avoid ships.** You'll have a tendency to rob them.

4 **Avoid picture frames.** You might get trapped in one.

5 **Use your bandanas to blow your nose.** That way, you'll be slightly less likely to put them on your head.

6 **Make a map that leads to your house.** Follow it and stay in bed for a day or two.

HOW TO REMOVE BARNACLES (FROM YOURSELF)

1 **Do not attempt to remove the barnacles with threats, hammers, or loud music.** These just make them hold on tighter. And a whack with a hammer can really smart.

2 **Find the end of the barnacle that's attached to you.** The other end is known as the "waving around" end.

3 **Place your fingers next to the barnacle and press down until your fingers are a couple of inches below the barnacle.**

4 **Slide your fingers under the barnacle and forcefully flick it away.**

5 **Move away before the barnacle reattaches itself.**

6 **Consider getting a job or a hobby.** If barnacles are attaching themselves to you, then you're not exactly Mr. or Ms. Action.

If The Barnacles Are Attached to You Somewhere You Can't Reach

1 **Call your very best friend in the whole wide world.**

2 **Ask him or her to perform Steps Two through Five above.**

3 **See Step Six yourself.**

if The Barnacles Are Only Attached to the Lower Half of Your Face

1 Those aren't barnacles— they're whiskers. You need a shave.

CHAPTER SIX:

SCHOOL SURVIVAL

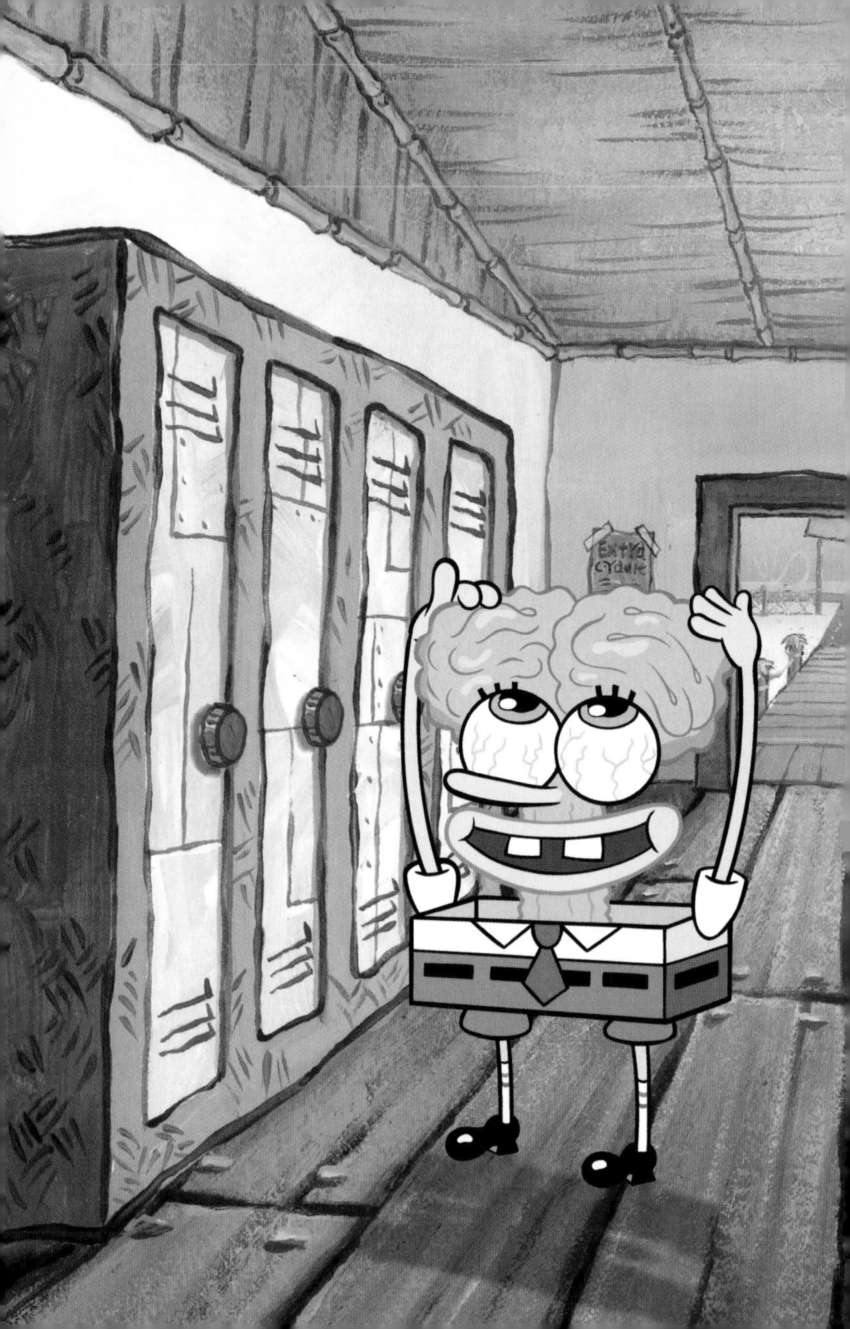

HOW TO SURVIVE A POP QUIZ

BY SPECIALIST Mrs. Puff

1 Don't panic. If you panic, you'll just start snapping pencils and flying around the room and driving me crazy like a certain sponge I know.

2 Don't ask if the quiz is about your father. It isn't.

3 Don't ask if the quiz is about soda. It's not.

4 Don't ask if the quiz is about firecrackers. NO, IT'S NOT! STOP ASKING THESE SILLY QUESTIONS! JUST TAKE THE QUIZ!

5 Take out your pencil, calmly read the questions, and answer them all correctly. Oh, if only my students would do this, I wouldn't have to spend every evening lying down with a cold cloth on my forehead.

6 Quietly turn your quiz in to the teacher. Don't do a "dance of triumph." Don't try to bribe the teacher. And don't immediately ask, "Did I pass, Mrs. Puff? Huh? Did I? Did I? Did I pass?"

7 It's really very simple—just use your brain!

HOW TO SURVIVE ART CLASS

BY SPECIALIST Squidward Tentacles

1 **The first thing to do is make sure you choose a class with a brilliant instructor.** Like me.

2 **Bring the proper materials.** You'll need a sketch pad, charcoal, paint, canvases, paint brushes, an easel, a palette, clay, marble, a chisel, a hammer, a smock, and a beret.

3 **Follow the rules of art.** Art is not about messing around, doing whatever you want. It's about following the laws of perspective, proportion, and color. And praising the teacher.

4 Quietly wait for the teacher to tell you what to draw or sculpt. You should be seated, with your hands folded on your desk.

5 Draw or sculpt the assigned subject.
EXACTLY THE WAY THE TEACHER TELLS YOU.

6 Listen as the teacher tells you what's wrong with your art. There'll be plenty, believe me.

7 Admit the teacher is a much better artist than you.
You should probably just stick to blowing bubbles.

HOW TO SURVIVE GYM CLASS

BY SPECIALIST SpongeBob SquarePants

Be Aware

If you're like me—in TOP physical condition—you'll have no trouble in gym class. But just in case, here are a few tips to help you get by.

1 Make friends with your gym teacher. Say stuff like, "Isn't sweat the greatest?"

2 Find out what each class's activity will be in advance. That'll give you a chance to discover things about each game—like what the heck it is.

3 Spot the best athlete in class. It should be easy—he or she will be the one who looks like they know what they're doing. They'll also have a cool headband.

4 Do what they do, only better. Simple!

5 If it's too hard, stay out of the way. Every gym and ballfield has a quiet little corner that no one's paying much attention to. Find it and stay there.

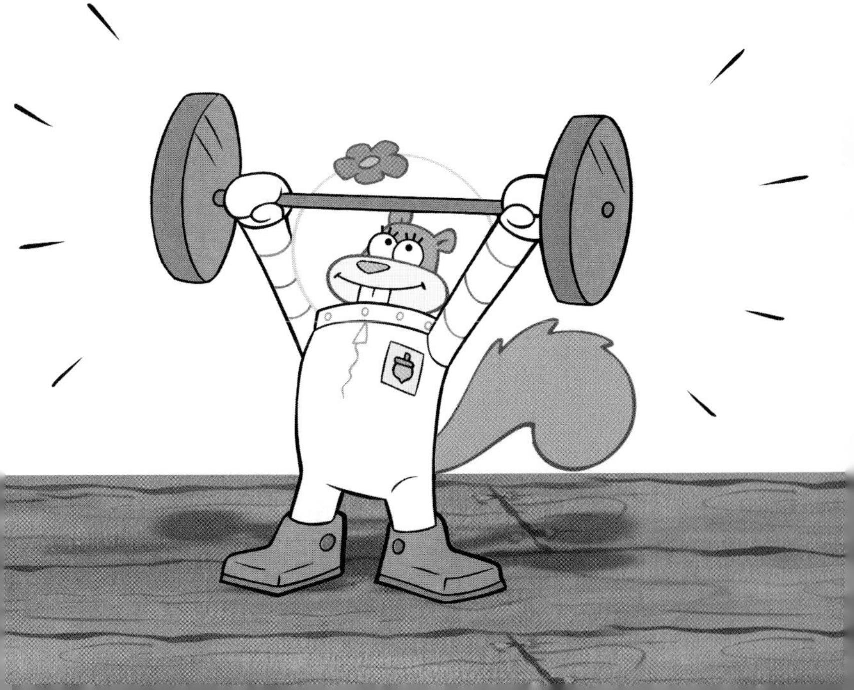

HOW TO SURVIVE BEING ON A SCHOOL TEAM

1 Go out for your school's worst team. You're sure to make it. If they keep losing, it's really not your fault. If they start winning, you can take credit.

2 Find out which position the coach's kid played in the past or will play in the future. That's the safest position to play. Of course, if the kid's playing it *now,* you'll never get it.

3 If you just want the glory of being on the team, try to get injured early in the season during practice. That way, you can just sit on the bench and enjoy yourself.

HOW TO WIN A RACE

BY SPECIALIST Patrick Star

1 Run faster than the other guy.

2 HA HA! I WIN! I WIN!

HOW TO TELL
IF A BUBBLE LIKES YOU

1 The bubble "just happens" to keep floating by your house.

2 Whenever you walk by the bubble and its friends, they all giggle.

3 At Mrs. Puff's Boating School, the bubble passes you a note that says, "Somebody likes you."

4 You see little heart-shaped bubbles above the bubble's head.

5 **Someone keeps stealing your soap.** You get the idea that someone doesn't want other bubbles in your house.

6 When you go jellyfishing, the bubble pretends to be a jellyfish.

7 You've never heard the bubble say a single bad thing about you.

8 It puts itself between you and the tough, mean bubbles.

9 Whenever you're around, the bubble seems to be floating on air.

Bubble Body Language

★ PERFECTLY ROUND = content, relaxed

★ PINCHED AT THE WAIST = tense, nervous

★ SPINNING = giddy, excited

★ BUMPING YOU = friendly or near-sighted

★ FLOATING = attentive, interested

★ NOT FLOATING = depressed

★ COVERED IN RAINBOWS = clean

★ INVISIBLE = popped

HOW TO SURVIVE A SCHOOL DANCE

BY SPECIALIST Sandy Cheeks

1 Golldurn it, I don't really see what all the fuss is about. A dance is just a dance. You know, a barn dance, a shebang, a hootenanny? A chance to kick up your heels!

2 If you're a feller, and you like a gal, just go up to her and ask if she wants to dance. If she says yes, grab her hand and head for the dance floor!

3 If you're a gal, and you like a feller, just go up to him and ask if he wants to dance. If he says yes, grab his hand and head for the dance floor. If he says no, do it anyway! (Lots of fellers are shy.)

4 Listen to the music and start dancin' like a buckin' bronco with a burr under his saddle!

HOW TO DEAL WITH A BULLY

1 **If you're a sponge, relax.** Just absorb the bully's punches with your spongy body until he's exhausted.

2 **If you're not a sponge, try intimidation.** Get your friends to talk loudly about how tough you are. Wear a "Boy, Am I Tough" T-shirt. Put on big fake inflatable arms.

3 **If the bully still wants to fight, run.** If he's that eager to fight, he must be good at it.

CHAPTER SEVEN:
HOUSE SURVIVAL

HOW TO TELL IF YOUR HOUSE IS ROTTING

BY SPECIALIST SpongeBob SquarePants

1 Everybody asks, "Say, do you have a rotting pineapple in your pocket?"

2 When you try to hang up pretty pictures, big chunks fall out of your walls.

3 The label on the back of your house says "Freeze or move out of by October 1998."

4 On windy days, people have to dodge pieces of your house.

5 Instead of using the mailbox, the mailman just shoves your mail right through the wall.

6 Your house smells worse than Patrick's laundry basket.

7 To reach the roof, all you have to do is stand on tiptoe.

8 Wow—even nematodes don't want to eat it.

HOW TO TREAT A SEVERED LIMB

If You're A Sponge

★ Just stick it back in—good as new!

If You're A Starfish

★ Just grow it back—good as new!

If You're An Octopus

★ Who cares? There's plenty more where that came from.

HOW TO GET OUT OF BED

1 When your extra-loud foghorn alarm goes off, wake up. To wake up, you should stop dreaming about Krabby Patties and open your eyes.

2 Fool your bed by turning over and saying, "Oh, I think I'll just stay in bed all day." Do *not* rub your eyes and stretch. Your bed'll know you're planning to get up.

3 Fling back your covers. Don't worry if they fall on the floor. You can pick them up later.

4 Scramble to your feet and stand on your bed.

5 Start jumping up and down on the bed. This isn't the only way to get out of bed, but it's the most fun.

6 Bounce so high that you can touch the ceiling. Then use your hands to push off the ceiling *at a sharp angle.*

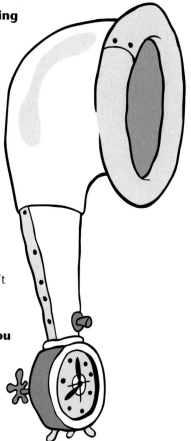

7 **Land on the floor.** If your sheets and blankets are on the floor, be sure to land *away* from them, so you don't get all tangled up, lie down, and fall back asleep.

8 **Run away from your bed, yelling "I'm up! I'm up! There's no way I'm going back to bed!"** Yell in a sincere, convincing tone so you'll believe what you're saying.

How to Prepare

AN EXTRA-LOUD ALARM CLOCK: We recommend a modified (to be even louder) foghorn, but you can also rig a clock with a fire alarm, a jackhammer, or a circus band.

SLIPPERY SHEETS: You want sheets you can slip right out of, so get some made out of eelskin or banana peels. Be sure to keep them well-greased.

TRAINED PET: Teach your pet to start biting you the second your alarm goes off.

PLENTY OF LIQUIDS: At night, just before you go to sleep, drink at least fourteen gallons of water.

HOW TO DEAL WITH SLEEP DEPRIVATION

BY GUEST EXPERT, Patrick Star

1 Sleep is very important. Whenever you get the chance, you should try to fall...zzzzzzzzzzzzzzzzzzzz.

12 Huh? Whaz...? Where am I?

49 Sleep is very...zzzzzzzzzzzzzzzzzzzzzzz.

K Who said that? Where? Show yourself, and I'll... zzzzzzzzzz.

6 Okay, if you're not getting enough sleep, the important thing is to...

119 ...um...

C ...oh, yeah. To go to sleep!

2G I recommend getting at least twenty-three hours of sleep a day, plus a one-hour nap.

L But if you're having trouble falling asleep, then you should...

5 + **3** ...um...

84R ...listen to something really boring. Like maybe a set of directions on how to do something. That's usually pretty...zzzzzzzzzzzzzzzzzzzz.

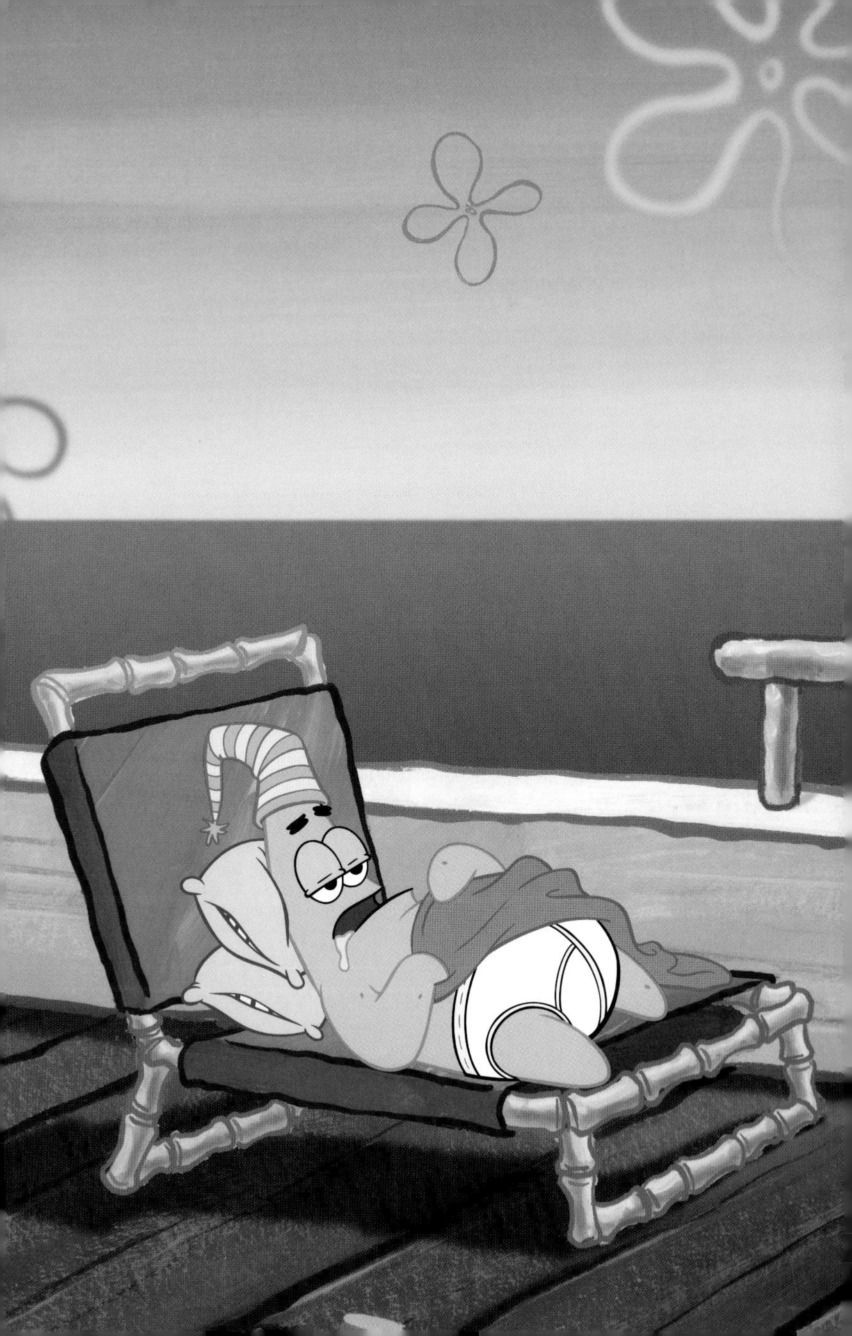

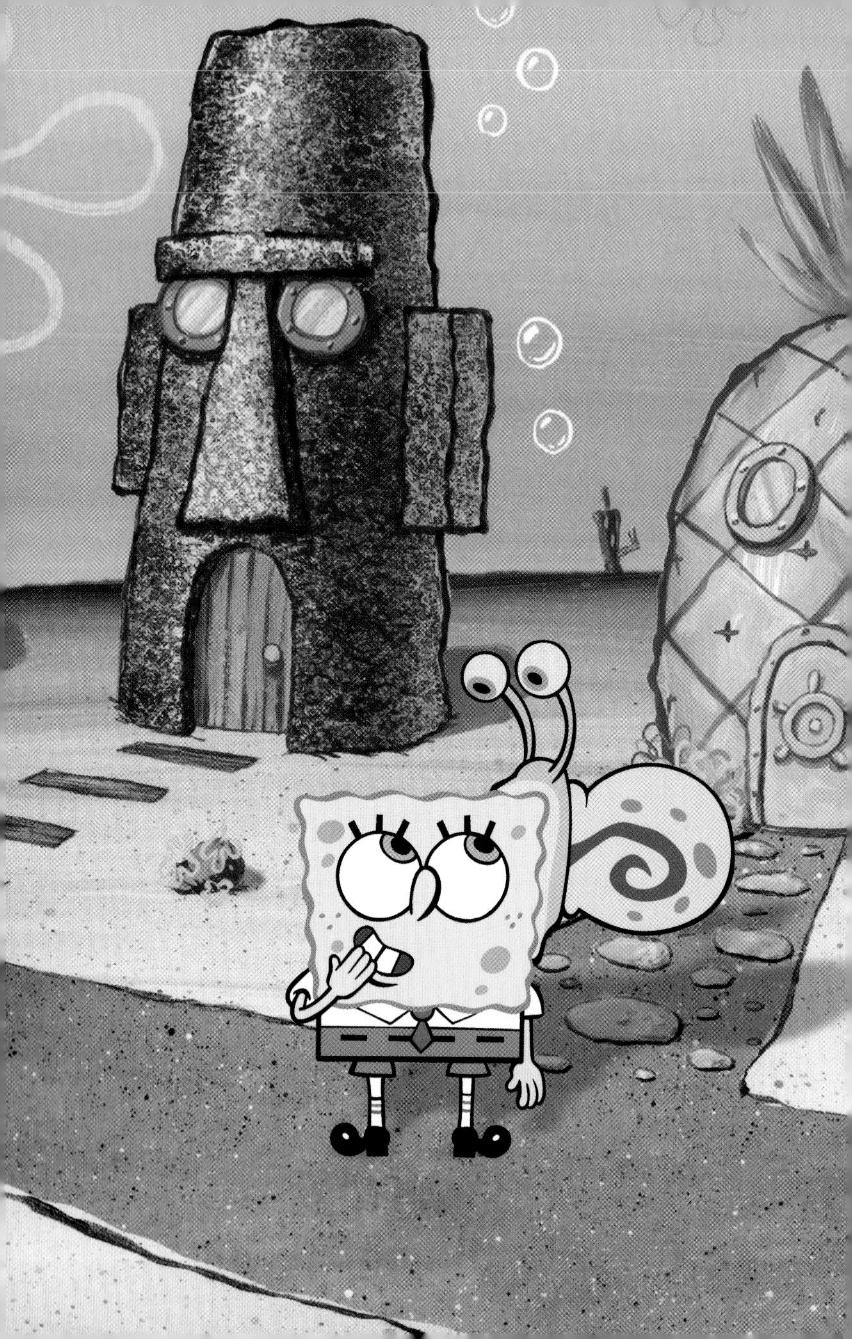

HOW TO TELL WHEN IT'S TIME FOR A NEW SHELL

DEDICATED TO SHELL SPECIALIST Gary

1 Every time you take a deep breath, you hear a crackling sound.

2 When you pull into your shell, about eighty percent of you is still out.

3 Most mornings you don't even bother to put it on.

4 When you got your current shell, land animals were just starting to evolve.

5 There's so much algae on your shell people mistake you for a bush.

6 Shell catalogs give up and take you off their mailing lists.

7 You can't fit your record player in there anymore.

8 Mr. Krabs gives you the money to buy a new shell.

Alternatives to Getting a New Shell

★ Become a nudist. You'll be vulnerable, but quicker.

★ Punch some holes in a discarded appliance box.

★ Move into a cave and hope you'll grow into it.

HOW TO SURVIVE A HAUNTING

1 Avoid the ghost. If your house is big enough, you can stay away from the ghost by never going in the haunted rooms again.

2 If your house isn't that big, you'll have to confront the ghost. Try to choose a time when the ghost isn't invisible. Or rattling chains. Or shrieking. It makes it hard to talk.

3 Don't say "boo" to the ghost. It doesn't scare them. It just encourages them to boo you back.

4 Tell the ghost it's a ghost. Most ghosts don't know this, which is weird, since all they have to do is look in the mirror.

5 Once the ghost knows it's a ghost, suggest it go somewhere creepier. Like a graveyard. Or an abandoned house. Or the Chum Bucket.

6 If the ghost thinks your house is plenty creepy, it's time for a new coat of paint. Pour it over the ghost. They really hate that.

CHAPTER EIGHT:

FINANCIAL SURVIVAL

HOW TO PROTECT YOUR MONEY

BY SPECIALIST Mr. Krabs

Be Aware

Oh, my money! How I love my beautiful, beautiful money! My money is like … money to me! It's so money! If you have some money, you might want to just give it to me. I'll give it a good home, and love it more than you ever could. Plus, I'll protect it.

1 Disguise your money.
Draw a mustache on all the presidents, so no one will recognize your money.

2 Teach your money never to talk to strangers.
Especially tax officials.

3 Make sure your money knows how to find its way home.
Take your money on walks, and point out the landmarks near your house. Like the bank, and the mint, and the money museum…

4 Sew tags into your money's clothing that say "Property of Mr. Krabs." You may think that your tags are supposed to read, "Property of [YOUR NAME]." But that's wrong. They should read, "Property of Mr. Krabs."

5 Memorize the serial numbers on all your bills.

6 Brand your coins with your own personal brand.
Sure, it stings 'em a little, but someday they'll thank you.

7 Lock your money in a vault with a secret combination that you don't tell ANYONE.

8 Lock your money vault in a vault vault.

9 Lock your vault vault in a vault vault vault.

10 Don't bother to shop for a vault vault vault vault.
They don't exist…yet.

Fun Things to Do With Your Money

★ Count it. Sometimes, when I'm almost done counting, I distract myself on purpose, so I'll have to start all over again.

★ Bathe in it. There's nothing more refreshing than a nice, cool money bath.

★ Build a fort with it. But *don't* get carried away and start throwing money balls.

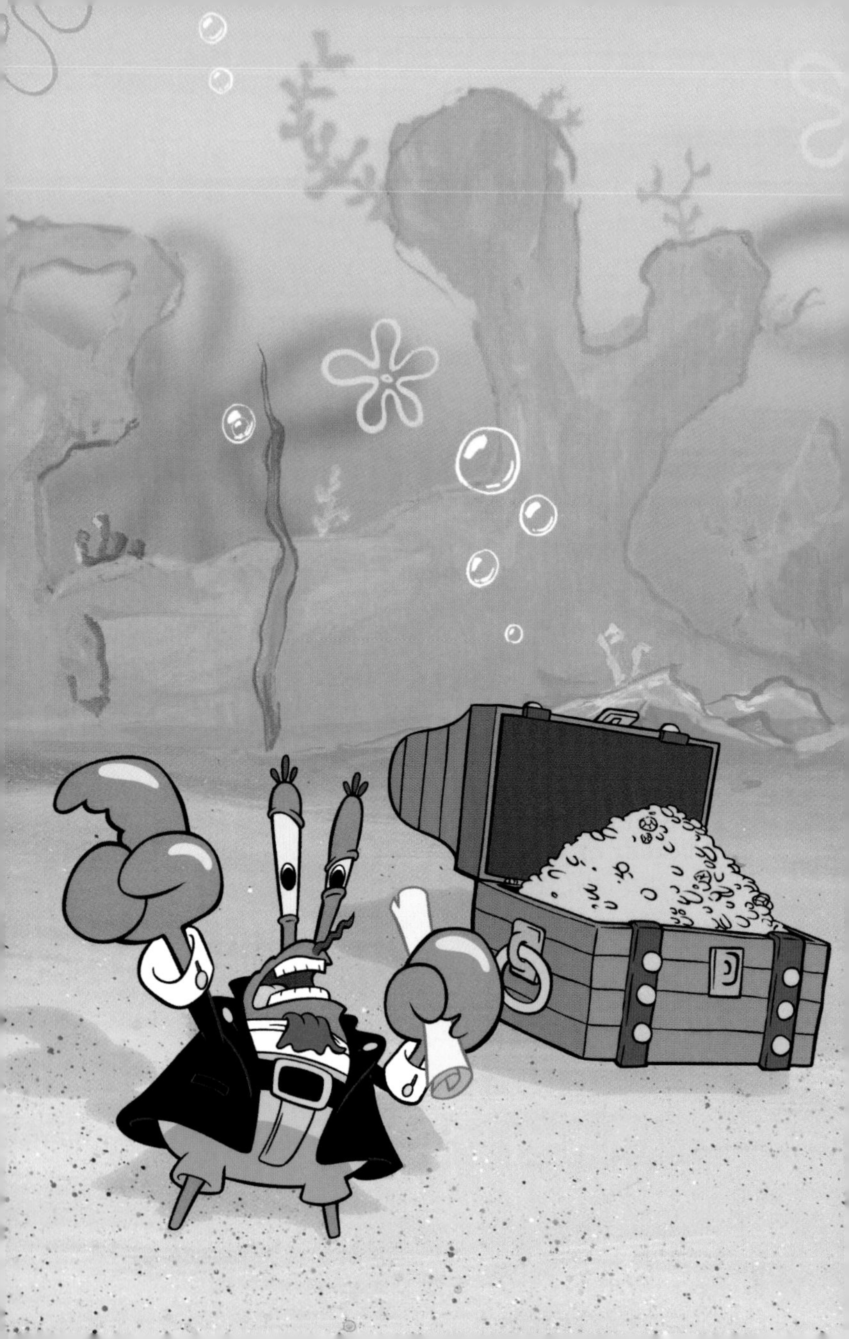

WHAT TO DO WITH A TREASURE CHEST

Finding One

1 Lift with your leg muscles. Since they're full of gold and jewels, treasure chests tend to be heavy, and if you're not careful, you could easily throw your back out. No amount of treasure is worth a sore back.

2 Drag the chest away from the spot you found it. Don't pause to open the chest right there on the spot. Pirates could show up any minute to reclaim their booty.

3 Break the lock off with a hammer and a chisel. Don't bother to go back and dig around for the key. Pirates almost *never* bury the key right next to the treasure chest. Except for maybe Dumbbeard the Pirate. But he never buried much treasure—mostly just expired coupons and old socks.

4 Before you break the lock off, make sure there isn't a curse on the chest. This probably should have been Step Three.

5 If there's no curse on the chest, open the lid. At this moment, there should be a chord of beautiful music and a yellow glow emanating from the chest. If there isn't, shut the lid and go hire a band and a lighting expert.

6 Take out the treasure, and immediately deposit it in a savings account with interest compounded *daily*. Remember: the stock market is much too risky for your buried treasure.

Hiding One

1 Find a deserted place in the middle of nowhere. Not the edge of nowhere, or halfway between the edge and the middle of nowhere, but in the *middle* of nowhere.

2 Dig a deep hole. The hole has to be big enough to hold the treasure chest. Otherwise, you're completely wasting your time.

3 Lower the chest into the hole. Remember, take the weight on your *legs,* not your *back.*

4 Cover the chest back up with the sand you dug out of the hole. This is very important. There's really no point in putting a treasure chest in a hole if you're not going to cover the chest up.

5 Place a large "X" over the spot where you buried the chest. Once you lose your map to the chest, this will help whoever finds it dig up the chest.

6 Walk home, counting your steps as you go. Make notes. For example, "Twenty paces west of the old sunken ship," "One-hundred paces past the quickly swimming fish," etc.

7 Referring to your notes, write out the directions *in reverse.* Otherwise, you've got directions from the buried treasure to your house.

8 Draw a map based on the reversed directions. Remember to include the "X."

9 Lose the map. You don't have to do this right away. Years and years may pass. But eventually, you've got to lose it, so someone else can find it and dig up the treasure. That's just how it works with treasure chests. No one digs up their *own* buried treasure.

HOW TO FOIL A FAST-CHANGE SCAM ARTIST

BY SPECIALIST Squidward Tentacles

1 Trust no one. Anyone can be a fast-change scam artist—an old man, a kid, a lady, that guy with the "I LUV SCAMMIN'" T-shirt ...

2 As soon as a customer starts to pay, go into super-alert, hyper-vigilant mode. This is when the scam will start.

Be Aware
When you've worked a cash register as long as I have, you've seen every scam in the book. Or at least one: the fast-change scam, where the con artist tries to trick you out of extra change.

3 When you take the customer's money, identify it out loud. For example, you might say, "Oh, I see you've given me a TWENTY-DOLLAR BILL. Just let me get the change for your TWENTY-DOLLAR BILL, the one you paid me with when you handed me TWENTY DOLLARS, Mister PAY-WITH-A-TWENTY-DOLLAR BILL."

4 Listen for clues.
You'll know the customer is trying to pull a fast-change scam if he or she then says any of the following:

★ "Um, I only gave you five dollars."

★ "Wait, I think I have a penny…"

★ "Could you please hurry up? I'm really hungry."

★ "Why do you keep saying 'twenty-dollar bill' so loud?"

5 Say, "Ah ha!" You can add, "I knew it!" if it feels right. It almost always does.

6 Take back the customer's food.

7 Hold onto the money as evidence.

8 Push the alarm button under the counter, summoning the police.

9 Point at the customer and scream, "FAST-CHANGE SCAM ARTIST! FAST-CHANGE SCAM ARTIST! FAST-CHANGE SCAM ARTIST!" This is kind of hard to say, so you might want to practice on some regular customers.

10 Hand the disgusting criminal over to the police.

11 Ask if there's a reward. And if there is, don't share it with Mr. Krabs, even if he threatens to fire you. He won't. Who else is he going to get to do your lousy job?

HOW TO ASK YOUR BOSS FOR A RAISE

1 **Approach with stealth.** When he's in his office lair, the boss can sense your desire for more money. If you don't sneak up on him, he's liable to disappear just when you've worked up the nerve to talk to him.

2 **Smile, giggle, and do a little dance.** This will confuse him.

3 **Gradually work dollar-sign motions into your dance.** This will subtly introduce the topic of money.

4 **Do your best imitation of a cash register.** This will unsubtly continue the topic of money.

5 **Pull out your empty pockets, shrug, and make a "sad clown" face.** If he laughs and applauds at this point, it's going to be tough.

6 **Ask without using the word "raise."** Bosses are programmed to hunch up their backs, raise their claws, and hiss when the word "raise" is mentioned. Say that you'd like a modest amplification of your occupational remuneration.

7 **While he sits there looking puzzled, explain that "amplification" means you'd like more . . .**

8 **...of what "remuneration" means, which is...**

9 **(Whisper this part)...money.**

10 **As he attacks you, bop him in the gills, which are very sensitive.**

11 **Then run out.** Just be grateful you have a job!

Kinds of Bosses to Watch out For

★ **THE NODDING SMILER:** nods and smiles, then does the opposite of what you ask

★ **THE SMILING NODDER:** very similar to the Nodding Smiler

★ **THE JUST-A-MINUTER:** keeps taking phone calls and meetings with other people while you're trying to talk to him

★ **THE DOGFISH:** starts growling and barking at you the minute he senses you're going to ask for more money

★ **THE LECTURER:** when you ask for a raise, answers with a long lecture about how he got started in the business, and how hard times are, and what he likes to do on the weekends, and what he's thinking about buying with the money he's not going to give you, until you sneak out of his office

HOW TO PUT YOUR ARCHRIVALS OUT OF BUSINESS (UNSUCCESSFULLY)

BY SPECIALIST (IN HIS OWN MIND) Plankton

1 Make sure you're well-fed. It takes a lot of energy to destroy someone else's business. I recommend a steady diet of diatoms, dinoflagellates, and foraminifers.

2 Spy on the competition. Put on a disguise and sneak into the business across the street. Your disguise doesn't have to be elaborate—holding your finger under your nose as a fake mustache will do nicely.

3 Find out what their best-selling item is. There are two excellent ways to do this. One is to notice what everybody's buying. The other is to go up to an employee and slyly ask, "Say, pal, what's your best-selling item?"

4 Discover how they _make_ their best-selling item. This is the trickiest part. They're not going to want you to find out their secret formula—that's why they call it a _secret_ formula, you idiot! You're going to have to use cunning. You're going to have to use guile. And you're going to have to use a big hammer to break through a window to sneak in at night and steal the formula.

5 Copy their best-selling item and give it a better name. Something with "ultra" in it. Or "mega." Or "super-dee-duper." Or "skull-crushing."

6 Sell the renamed item for one penny less than your competitor. Oh, that's clever!

7 Sell so many of the renamed items that you DRIVE YOUR CRUMMY COMPETITORS OUT OF BUSINESS FOREVER! Oh, HA HA HA HA HO HO HEE HEE HO HA! (That's an *evil* laugh, by the way, not a jolly one.)

8 If you manage to do this, tell me how. I've never managed to do it myself...yet!

CHAPTER NINE:
WILDERNESS SURVIVAL

HOW TO FIND YOUR WAY TO THE KRUSTY KRAB WITHOUT A COMPASS

What You Won't Need

★ A compass

Sniff Method

1 **Stick your nose up in the air.**

2 **Take a *big* sniff.**

3 **Smell that delicious smell that smells smelly? Not smelly like an anchovy, but smelly like good food?** That's the smell of Krabby Patties! Made only at the Krusty Krab!

4 Look for the curly, white "smell smoke" that's going in your nose. Anytime you smell something really delicious, you'll see that smoke.

5 Follow the smell smoke back to the Krusty Krab. And order a Krabby Patty!

Listen Method

1 Cup your hand around your ear.

2 Take a _big_ listen.

3 Try to hear people saying things like "Oh, boy, is this good," "This is the best thing I ever ate," and "Yumm mm mm mmm gulp chew bite mmm yum!"

4 Walk in the direction that makes those voices get louder and louder.

5 Before you know it, you'll be at the Krusty Krab!

Yell Method

1 Cup your hands around your mouth.

2 As loudly as you can, yell, "HEY, LOOK, SOMEBODY DROPPED A NICKEL!"

3 Wait for Mr. Krabs to coming running up.

4 Follow him back to the Krusty Krab!

HOW TO FIND YOUR WAY OUT OF AN UNDERSEA CAVE

If You Can See the Mouth of the Cave From Where You're Standing

1 **Walk out of the mouth of the cave.**

If You Can't See the Mouth of the Cave, But You Have a Flashlight

1 **Shine the flashlight around until you see the mouth of the cave.**

2 **Walk out of the mouth of the cave.**

If You Can't See the Mouth of the Cave and You Don't Have a Flashlight

1 **Close your eyes.** This will make not being able to see less upsetting.

2 **Stick your hands out straight in front of you.**

3 **Walk.** When your hands touch a cave wall, turn and walk in a different direction.

4 **While you're walking, call out, "Mouth of the cave, where are you?"** Walk *away* from the echo.

Be Aware
Many undersea caves have horrible monsters in them. There's nothing you can do about this, but you should be aware of it.

5 **Cave water is colder than non–cave water, so if you feel warmer water, walk toward it.** Unless you just took a bathroom break.

6 **If you suddenly see light, that means you've opened your eyes.** Close them again.

7 **Keep walking until you're out of the cave.**

8 **If you can't find your way out, keep your eyes closed and play your nose like a flute.** It won't help you find the mouth of the cave, but it'll make you feel better.

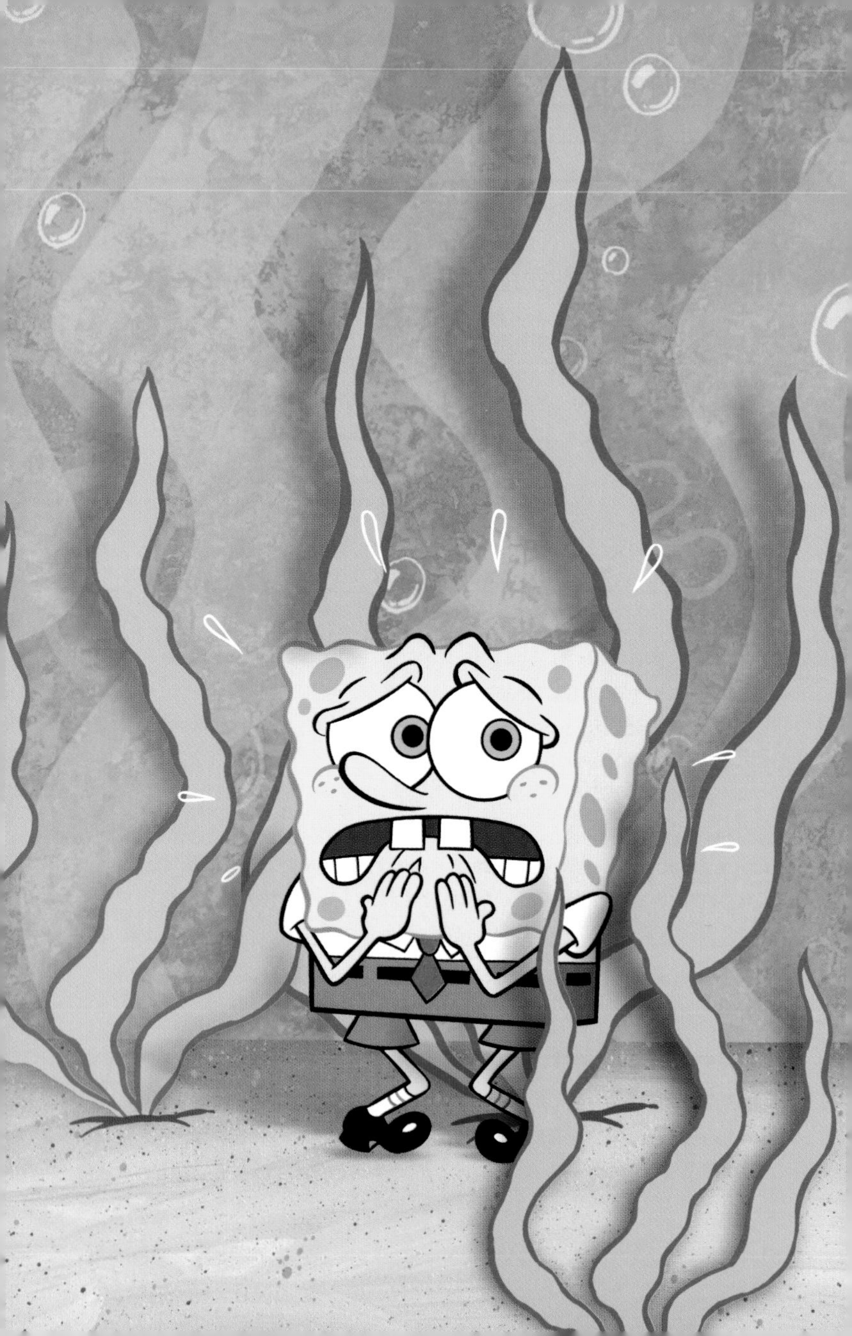

HOW TO SURVIVE BEING LOST IN A KELP FOREST

How to Find Your Way Back to Bikini Bottom

1 Just sit down and wait to be rescued. They're sure to come find you eventually! They'll miss you! A lot!

2 If you haven't got time to wait, turn around and walk back *exactly* the way you came in. It helps if you say everything you said on the way in, only backward.

3 If you're still lost, scream "GET YOUR HOT, FRESH, DELICIOUS KRABBY PATTIES HERE!" Someone will run up, wanting to eat a Krabby Patty, and they'll know the way to the Krusty Krab, which is in Bikini Bottom!

4 If no one runs up to help, write "This Way to Bikini Bottom" on a sign. Stick it in the ground where it looks the most natural. Then walk in the direction it's pointing.

How to Avoid Getting Lost in the Kelp Forest

1 Don't go in the kelp forest.

HOW TO FiND WATER iN THE OCEAN

1 Look in unlikely places. It's always where you least expect it—in the oven, at the back of your sock drawer, stuck to the inside of the dryer...

2 Listen for flowing water. Then follow the sound to the source of that water. There may be water there.

3 Scan the area for stuff that's floating. Once you find something floating, check to see what it's floating in. Nine times out of ten, it's water. Of course, sometimes it's pudding.

4 Take a big sniff. If water goes up your nose, then you've found water.

5 Find a blooming flower. Dig the flower up. Now wave it around. If you see bubbles, chances are you're surrounded by water.

6 Check your pockets. You think you've already checked all your pockets, but sometimes pockets have little pockets inside them. And there's almost always a pocket in your jacket that you've forgotten about.

7 Throw a rock. Wait until it lands. If you hear a splashing sound, you've found yourself somewater, my friend.

Be Aware
Water can be shy. Sometimes it just doesn't want to be found. In that case, you should leave the water alone for a while, and then approach it very quietly. Wave at it, smile, and talk about something it's interested in, like currents. Then drink it.

HOW TO SURVIVE BEING LOST IN YOUR HOUSE

BY SPECIALIST Patrick Star

1 It's easy to get lost in your own house.

7 I've done it hundreds of times.

4 Here's what you should do.

2 Reach out and grab something.

38 Look at the thing you grabbed.

B **See if you recognize it.** Is it your TV? Your refrigerator? Your box of crackers?

3 **Once you recognize the thing, ask yourself, "Now, where do I keep this thing?"**

Q Pause for a snack.

159 **Pause for another snack.** Because this is hard work—remembering stuff.

12 **Eventually, maybe you'll remember where you keep the thing you're holding.** Then you'll know where you are in your house.

F **If not, just start watching TV, and you'll probably forget that you're lost.**

9 **It's easy.** I forget stuff all the time.

P What was I saying?

How to Avoid Getting Lost in Your Own House

1 Huh?

2 How should I know?

3 The end.

4 By Patrick.

5 Wow, I'm an author!

CHAPTER TEN:
DANGEROUS SURVIVAL

HOW TO ESCAPE FROM A POOL OF TARTAR SAUCE

1 When walking in tartar sauce country, always carry empty tartar sauce packets. They just might save your life.

2 As you start to sink into the tartar sauce, slowly pull the empty packets out of your pockets. If you pull them out too fast, tartar sauce will pour into your pockets, and you'll sink even faster.

3 Hold the empty packets open and yell, "Get in there, tartar sauce!" You may have to yell this several times. Don't worry—just keep yelling, and eventually the tartar sauce will get the idea.

4 As the tartar sauce climbs into the packets and fills them, toss them away, one by one.

5 Once all the tartar sauce is in packets, walk away from the packets, taking the shortest route possible. Be careful not to step on the packets. The tartar sauce could squish out. Plus, you'll slip and bonk your head.

Be Aware
If you can gather *all* the pickle chunks, the pool won't be tartar sauce—it'll just be a harmless pool of mayonnaise.

if You Don't Have Any Empty Tartar Sauce Packets with You

1 You're doomed.

2 Don't bother moving on to Step Two, because you are doomed. And no, little paper cups won't work.

3 Look, we said you're doomed. Aren't you listening?

4 Okay, you're right—there's always another way.

Alternative Method

1 While your eyes are still above the top of the pool, quickly scan the surface for a chunk of diced pickle. The pickle chunks are the green things in the tartar sauce.

2 Using all your strength, swim toward that pickle chunk.

3 Grab the pickle chunk.

4 Look around for another pickle chunk.

5 Swim toward it. Bring the first pickle chunk with you.

6 Grab the second pickle chunk.

7 Keep collecting pickle chunks until you have enough to fashion a pickle boat.

8 Fashion a pickle boat.

9 Climb into it, and sail out of the tartar sauce.

HOW TO SURVIVE BEING HOOKED

BY SPECIALIST Mr. Krabs

1 **Yell, "OH, IT'S A TERRIBLE THING BEING HOOKED!"**
It won't help, but it'll make you feel better.

2 **Grab that crummy hook.** But not by the hook part, or you'll hook your hand. Grab the other end.

3 **Pull the hook out.**

4 **Let the hook go.** It'll go flying back up to the awful, bright, shiny top of the sea.

5 **Come to the Krusty Krab for a Krabby Patty with the works!** It'll cure what ails ya!

6 **No, it's not on the house!**
What are you—nuts?

HOW TO SURVIVE AN UNDERWATER VOLCANO ERUPTION

1 If you live on top of a volcano, stay alert at all times. Watch for the subtle signs of eruption: booming sounds, lava falling everywhere, a bright orange glow in the middle of the night, the water around you starting to boil, etc.

2 If you're in your house, go to an upper floor and hide under the bed. Unless your house is built on top of a volcano. Then you should get the heck out of there.

3 Run away from the volcano as fast as you can. Do not run half as fast as you can, or even almost as fast as you can, but *as fast as you can.* It's also important not to run *faster* than you can, because that defies logic. The last thing you want to do during a volcano explosion is defy logic.

4 If you have a fireproof umbrella, put it up.

5 Run in a zigzag pattern to confuse the volcano. To confuse it even more, run in a zag-zig pattern.

6 **If the volcano starts to chase you, there's a simple solution.** Run faster.

7 **No, wait a minute. You're already running as fast as you can.**

8 **Um...**

9 **If the volcano starts to chase you, use your pants as a net to catch a bunch of jellyfish, and then float away.** Very few volcanoes can fly.

What Not to Do

★ Don't try to make friends with the volcano.

★ Don't hide from the volcano in a dry haystack.

★ Don't run *toward* the volcano.

★ Don't dive *into* the volcano.

★ Don't stand around saying, "Gee, 'volcano.'
   That's a funny word. I wonder where it came from..."

★ Don't start a game of "Lava, lava, who's got the lava."

HOW TO ESCAPE FROM A BUBBLE

1 Make sure you really are trapped inside a bubble, and not just looking out a window. Remember: if you're in a bubble, there should be shiny clear stuff *all around you*, not just in front of you.

2 Ask the bubble to please let you out. Be polite. Bubbles' feelings are easily hurt. They have very thin skins.

3 If the bubble won't let you out, check to see if there's a bubble door. If there is a bubble door, open it and exit the bubble.

4 If there's no door, look for the bubble's weak spots. A seam, for example, can be a weak spot. Unfortunately, almost no bubbles have seams.

5 Once you've found a weak spot, gently try to pry it open.

6 If gentle prying fails, kick and karate-chop the weak spot as hard as you can.

7 **As soon as you break through the bubble's weak spot, get out and run as far away from the bubble as possible. While you're running, scream.**

How to Avoid Getting Caught in a Bubble in the First Place

★ If you're blowing bubbles, remember to keep the bubble wand *out of your mouth.*

★ Always blow the bubbles *out.* Never suck them *in.*

★ After you blow a really big bubble, resist the urge to climb inside it.

★ When you're getting in a taxi, first check to make sure it's not a bubble pretending to be a taxi.

★ At night, always drool. Otherwise you might wake up inside a spit bubble.

★ If you see a bubble coming right at you, duck.

Be Aware
Not every bubble is trying to trap you. Most bubbles are very friendly, and wouldn't hurt a sand flea. A good sign that a bubble is unfriendly is when it makes a scary face, growls, and yells, "I'm going to get you!" Or when it's Mermaid Man and Barnacle Boy's archvillain, The Dirty Bubble! Or both!

HOW TO SURVIVE TRIPPING

BY SPECIALIST
SpongeBob SquarePants

if You Fall All the Way to the Ground

1 Try to land on something nice and soft, like your face.

2 Look around on the ground and say, "Oh, *here's* that pebble I was looking for! Found it!"

if You Don't Fall Down

1 Pretend you were just breaking into a run.

2 Break into a run.

3 This time, watch where you step.

HOW TO SURVIVE RIPPING YOUR PANTS

What You'll Need

* Needle
* Thread
* Measuring tape
* Sewing machine
* Book on how to sew
* Spare pair of pants

1 Pile the needle, thread, measuring tape, sewing machine, and book on how to sew in front of you so people can't see what you're doing.

2 Take off the ripped pants.

3 Put on the spare pants.

4 It's just that easy!

HOW TO SURVIVE BEING BARE

1 **Check to see if you are taking a shower or a bath.** If you are, being bare poses no danger. You can feel free to start worrying about something else.

2 **If you are not taking a shower or a bath, check to see if you are in public.** If you're in the privacy of your own home, you may still be able to get away with being bare.

3 **If you are in a public place, you need to take immediate steps to stop being bare.**

4 **Do NOT climb a tree.** This will just call attention to your bareness.

5 **Stay still.** Maybe people won't notice you.

6 **If you hear laughter, check to see if people are pointing at you.** If they are, try to cover their eyes.

7 **Get some clothes.** This step is extremely important.

8 **Put the clothes on.** Move quickly, but don't rush, or you'll just end up with a shirt on your head and your pants on backward. A good clue that you're rushing is that the laughter gets even louder.

9 **Fasten the clothes tightly.** Otherwise, you may still be in grave danger of being bare.

HOW TO SURVIVE WAITING IN LINE AT THE MOVIES

1 **Do not panic—eventually, the line *will* move.**

2 **Stay where you are.** Do not wander away. This is a sure way to lose your place in line.

3 **Concentrate on the person right in front of you.** Don't think about the person in front of that person, and the person in front of that person, and the person in front of that person...or you might LOSE YOUR MIND!

4 **Tie your shoes.** This will help pass the time, and when the line moves, you'll be ready to step forward. If your shoes are already tied, untie them. Then tie them. See how time is just flying by?

5 **If you're meeting someone, send up a flare to let them know where you are.**

6 Make sure you're in the right line. If you don't have tickets, make sure you're in the line to buy tickets. If you *do* have tickets, make sure you're in the line to see the movie. Actually, this is probably the first thing you should have done.

7 Organize a sing-a-long! This is a really fun way to pass the time. People love to sing in public with total strangers! Make a game of it—try to think of a song that would make a good theme song for the movie you're about to see. Of course, you haven't seen the movie yet, so you don't really know what it's about...but you could sing songs about waiting in line.

8 Conserve your energy. You don't know how long you might have to stand in this line, so don't exhaust yourself by jogging in place or doing jumping jacks. Save that for the line to the bathroom.

9 If it's night, build a campfire. It can get awfully dark and cold in a movie line. Besides, this way you can make s'mores!

10 Don't lose your ticket. Assuming you've already bought your ticket, it's very important to not lose it. Hold it out in front of you with both hands, saying, "I'm ready...to see a movie!"

HOW TO SURVIVE NEEDING TO GO TO THE BATHROOM

BY SPECIALIST Patrick Star

1 **Dance in place.** Jump back and forth from one foot to the other.

2 **Hold it...**

3 **Hold it...**

4 **Hold it...**

5 **Oh, just let it go...**

6 **AH! MUCH BETTER!**

HOW TO END A BOOK

BY SPECIALIST SpongeBob SquarePants

1 Make sure you've said everything you want to say. Or that you've run out of pages.

2 "The End" is always kind of nice. But that's really more for story books.

3 Some books end with an index. Which sounds kind of hard to make…

4 How about a section called "About the Specialists"?

5 YEAH!

ABOUT THE SPECIALISTS

Squidward Tentacles has been working as a cashier at the Krusty Krab for "way too long." As the neighbor of SpongeBob SquarePants, he knows all about how important privacy is. He is a member of Disgruntled Employees of Bikini Bottom, the Clarinet Society, and the Pessimists' Club.

Patrick Star lives under a rock. He has gotten lost in his house many, many times, and has spent more time sleeping than anyone else in Bikini Bottom or possibly even the ocean.

Mr. Krabs is the long-time owner, manager, and captain of the Krusty Krab. He is also the director and sole member of the Center for the Preservation of Penny-Pinching. His hobbies include coin collecting, coin counting, and coin kissing.

Plankton is the owner and petty tyrant of the Chum Bucket restaurant, and has been trying to put his arch-rival, the Krusty Krab, out of business for years. He has never succeeded. He never will.

Sandy Cheeks is a certified instructor of Extremely Frightening Aquatic Sports. She has successfully surfed typhoons, tsunamis, tornadoes, hurricanes, and of course, whirlpools. She is a member of the Squirrels Club, the Society to Prevent Boredom, and the Underwater Friends of Texas.

Mrs. Puff comes from a long line of puffer fish. She runs her own boating school, where her perpetual student SpongeBob SquarePants keeps her very familiar with being inflated and deflated.

SpongeBob SquarePants lives in a pineapple under the sea. Absorbent and yellow and porous is he.